Copyright © 2014 by Lillian Kruzsely

All rights reserved. This book or any portion thereof may not be reproduced or used in any manner whatsoever without express written permission of the publisher except for the use of brief quotations in a book review.

Printed with Blurb Inc.
San Francisco, California

Printed in the United States of America

LK Publishing
Ottawa, On
Canada

Affairs in Red

By Beth Turner

To playing the part well

Contents

Chapter 1	Introduction	1
Chapter 2	Previously	10
Chapter 3	Last Words	19
Chapter 4	Death Was in the Air	26
Chapter 5	Perspectives of Death	34
Chapter 6	Concerning the Devil	42
Chapter 7	The Immortality of the Soul	49
Chapter 8	The Element of Time	56
Chapter 9	Effects Within the Inconsistencies of Time	63
Chapter 10	On Human Nature	72
Chapter 11	Uncertainty	78
Chapter 12	Illness	83
Chapter 13	The Woman at the Hospital	90
Chapter 14	First Impressions	96
Chapter 15	Eyes	103
Chapter 16	Dialogue	109
Chapter 17	Untitled	121
Chapter 18	Aftermath	129
Chapter 19	A Reoccurring Dream	135
Chapter 20	Necessity	144
Chapter 21	A Strange Occurrence	150
Chapter 22	He Festered Within Every Crevice of My Life	156
Chapter 23	A Harder Lesson to Learn	167
Chapter 24	The Concept of Love	173
Chapter 25	Belief	180
Chapter 26	The Soul of the City	186
Chapter 27	Ghosts	190
Chapter 28	Tears	196
Chapter 29	Afterword	199
Chapter 30	Completion and Contemplation	202

Introduction

What I wouldn't do for even just an opportunity to make you as happy as you make me in your presence. When I'm with you I smile harder than I have ever remembered smiling before. Surely, I cannot attribute this to coincidence. Nor is it simply your terribly great looks that enthrall and move me in ways so unfamiliar to anything I've ever known before. It seemed to be something from another world, a truly strange and surreal occurrence. If ever some instance might exist that could add some sort of validity to the feeling one expresses from having met another being in a past life, I can say safely, that this is certainly the most accurate example I can offer.

To be the person whom the love story is written about or the person who is the writing cet story. Indeed such a question is really quite simple and easy to answer; it is simply personal preference. Either way, such situations were already actually meant to work out the way they were supposed to from the start. There's never anything you can do after the fact to change any sort of ending that has already occurred, as I am sure almost anyone can confirm. You will always have more than one option, but the one you end up with in the end might be the one you were meant to end up with. Until that is, such circumstances arise that allow for you to end up choosing the option that does not keeps you awake at night eternally wondering what you could have been done differently to alter the outcomes of your past actions. The other person then might be labelled as the catalyst that you could somewhat tangibly associate to any feelings of longing and completeness that were now being filled into your mind. Could the notion of true love be simply the notion of a soul that you are in the end, meant to be with? Often, I choose to believe that there is someone out there meant for everyone. Usually, I delve only into this notion on the nights that I do not feel loved. On the nights that I feel completely alone in the world where I am unable to think of anyone whom I believed to have cared about me as much as I would have about them had they given me the chance.

Curiously enough however, one night whilst I was up and awake, refusing to fall asleep into a shamefully miserable slumber that would surely have resulted in horrific dreams; I expanded on this idea instead. What is a soul but the character of the being that it embodies? A person by definition is constructed of three material things. A mind, a body, and a soul.

Often, a soul is regarded as a thing that cannot be measured because it is not something that can be seen. To say such a thing without any proof or lack of it is completely absurd. I would like to label this example as the very definition of such an injustice. Throughout our lives we see and meet so many different people, each and every one with many different expressions of character. A soul surely then, can be defined as the character that any selected person exudes. For example, if someone was constantly bubbly and upbeat, one could and would describe this being as being an upbeat soul, or a good person to be around. If someone was depressed constantly or difficult to be around, one might label this person as lost, or in other words, a sad soul. Throughout the many lives that we may or may not have had, the end result would be ultimately, to find our soul mate. When such an action then becomes fulfilled, our soul would no longer then require to exist any further and would be able to rest at last, with the other half of itself that was found in finding such a fulfiller. A soul then, being divided in half, would have no option of resting once its human embodiment seizes to exist if they did not find the other half in which they were given their body to find in the first place. Having said that, if a person dies, having not found their other half of soul, then the soul might move on to the next body, or onto its next life hoping again, with the end goal of finding its one and true eternal fulfiller.

I'd like to believe that if and when this happens, the soul having been completed, would no longer have any need to be a presence on the earth. This could very well be the goal of our existences as human beings on the earth.

Some argue that God does exist, perhaps he does, and perhaps he doesn't. I cannot argue about a subject to which I am not subjected to. A God is just that; an entity that is differentiated from a human through being superior or all knowing. As a human, God should not matter to us because no matter what we do concerning him, no solid conclusion can ever be made because we cannot investigate a subject that we are so distant from understanding. If a God was something that we could tangibly believe in, then I am implored to believe that some other form of representation other than an old scripture would be present to affirm our beliefs in such a concept.

Personally, I do not believe that a God exists, and as humans we should not put our power and faith into something that ultimately, will have never have any avail. We are humans for a reason. Let us be human as oppose to searching for a God, something that we can never truly understand. We are human to be ourselves, to create something for ourselves. We have able bodies, able minds, and able souls. We can make something for ourselves instead of relying and putting our faith into something so distant from our existence. I choose to put my faith in that of other people, because at least other humans are tangible beings that can either confirm or deny the faith that I put in them through their actions and how they affect me. But for the sake of this story, a God must exist. The Devil exists here, so God must serve only now as an equalizer within these pages.

Most individuals that aim to disagree with me on this point derive quite a large amount of their arguments from the base point that the belief in something that you cannot explain is the basis for what most religions preach. One of its purposes is to not have anything tangible to associate with it; it is simply all in the power of belief. Ultimately, this then becomes an extension of my viewpoint. It might just be my place in the world to refuse to believe the idea that believing in something that doesn't exist is the way through which someone would ultimately be saved in the end. Saved from what, I care not to know. Supposedly as the story goes, ones soul is the object that comes into question at the end of our bodies' existence on this earth. If we prove ourselves to have lived a good life in front of the eyes of God while we are on this earth, our soul would then be saved and brought to heaven. The judgment of all those souls seems a mighty task for one almighty entity to accomplish, especially when there are over seven billion people on this earth currently. The whole story to me just seems more than difficult to accept, but again, as I said, it could just be me.

If the goal of ones life is not then, to be labelled in its final judgment as either having had lived a good or bad life, then what might the goal be? The answer that holds water for me, at least currently in this lifetime, is the finding of one's soul mate. I have been blessed with poor health since I was but a small child and of course, also the poor misfortune of solitude that come along with having many physical ailments. Ever since I can remember, I have felt completely alone in the world, something I simply cannot explain. I have tried to understand the notion of love, and humbly, I have not been able to. Whether this means only that I have not found the right person yet or that I am simply as cold as the ice that courses through my veins, I am not sure. Somehow, I have found purpose in writing of late, only with the end goal of trying to forget someone which I believe could very well have been my one true love; my soul mate. And so it is here that our story begins.

I know for certain I would never have been able to write such a story without your sparkling presence in my life Vergil. Just like Leonardo da Vinci's most famous work; the Mona Lisa, you have inspired me like no other living being in the world has ever been able too, and I dare to say, will ever be able to. In your presence I seem simply to melt away, my physical existence fades away with time, melting the past into the future, becoming one with my thoughts and fantasies of a love that I have never known. Never before could I have ever imagined myself as having been able to accomplish such a great and meaningful task and I would like to attribute such an accomplishment to you. You shall exist in history, by my choice exclusively, as the only other person in this world that I can tangibly say I have loved. Lisa Gherardini would go on in history to die never knowing that she would go down as being known to be most viewed portrait in history. Her smile, like yours, whispers with hints of wonder, mysticism, and elusive ambiguity. I wish only for my work to resemble such a work of art as this. Although it is very possible that such a madam was not as enchanting in reality as she is depicted in the painting, it is the manner in which Leonardo chose for her to be remembered by that makes it such a notable piece. I wish for you only to remain as you are in this book forever, as you surely will.

Life has presented me with the opportunity to ferment you within the sands of time, a gift I find you more than suitable of receiving. I have never in my life before experienced something so upturning, and as noteworthy as you, my dearest Vergil. If I die before this volume is finished, then time has taken away from me something that I surely never had the chance of having to begin with. Death would only solidify such a notion. Even in a past life I believe that we could never have been together. However, in this one, I will be dammed if I shall not take my last breath trying to take you with me through history the best that I can. Never before has my heart skipped as many beats as it has in your presence. If I die never having been able to call you my own, then surely the human race will have a new definition for the word tragedy. You shall always have my heart Vergil and I have no problem spending the rest of my life doing everything in my power to have even one more chance to hold you in my arms, to hear the sound of your opalescent voice whispering in my ears, and to be loved, surely, as such a beautiful creature as yourself was meant to be loved. I wish to go down in history, in this life, as the one with the hope that one day I might be given the opportunity to make you as happy and inspired as you have made me.

Now, it does not seem a completely absurd notion to imagine for a moment that our lives have simply been pre-directed to a certain destination, and no matter what sort of catalysts or altering events occur to change our routes along the path, the end is one that we will always get to. You may choose whatever route you do, attack any problem employing your solving method of choice, but you will always have the experiences and stories that have defined your life no matter how it happens. The lessons you learn will have occurred no matter what altering catalysts were present when such a defining moment occurred. A crowning example of such a catalyst is a human being. For example if you had a defining life moment such as getting arrested with another person, surely it would then be you human nature to associate that person with the moment that ensued such an emotion to follow. In this example, the act of getting arrested would have been somewhat of a bonding experience for those whom it has occurred to. Now the notion of concluding that such a situation would be attributed to the personalities of the other persons or people involved and not the lesson that you learned from it does occur. What we don't realize actually is that these people, the ones that you learn the lesson with, do not matter. The lesson that is learned from any experience could have and would have been obtained through some other media or experience. And if the sentence "that's life" holds any water, like it has been doing exactly so in my life of late, then surely nothing new is really occurring that anyone has been interested in enough to note.

History has long been defined as the elements, usually social, political, economic, and environmental which comprise the past. Whatever percentage this may be true, war is a largely more suitable and universally applicable situation to what our human history is all about. Meaning that the period in history where war occurred has always been much more significant than a time period where no such events ever did occur. War is essentially history. If war ceases to occur, then history largely seizes to exist also. History remains only in the objects that we as humans put it into. Examples that perfectly demonstrate these ideas are different variants of expression. Things like a movie, a book, or a painting. They are all perfect examples of things that hold and exemplify history. As a result of the termination of the Second World War, the largest influx of artful documentation of expression had occurred in history. One could not sit down and read for their entire lifetime, and materialize with the end result of having learned and read all the materials present that can be associated with this war. The countless authors it inspired, the countless pieces of art it inspired, the countless movies that have been created, even up to this day, to serve as a form of expression of war; exist only because the Second World War did actually happen. I use this as an example only because it is one that is universally applicable because it was a war that occurred on a global scale. It holds no meaning within these pages other than to serve as an example, for it is also an event that holds a place in time.

As I sit here staring lifelessly at the clock, time seems to slip through my fingers, and not a moment passes that isn't spent thinking about you. It is here that my conflict with time has come to begin. Lately, the only way that sleep is able to find me is when I am lying in bed crying about how a deeper part of me misses you. Even when I dream, it is of you. You have taken over my existence as though you are an extension of me, and I exist only as an extension of you. When I awake in the morning, my eyes are closed shut by the tears I have cried, now dry from the night before, which confirmed only that I fell asleep longing for you, and that I awake only now, with the same purpose.

You fester in my mind as the most ingrained of my ailments, surpassing all of my other medical issues with your presence in my mind. It is nice, for once to think of something that is not working as an extension of my body to kill me, like most thing in my life are. Maybe you serve simply as an addition to my physical ailments, to serve only as the catalyst that will lead to my demise in the end. For the body, mind, and soul cannot exist when all three undergo constant disintegration. If that stands as the case, I must say that I do not mind such a demise. You deserve everything in the world, even if that includes my life. Presently it does not seem much like living either. The pain of not being able to be with you is physically unbearable.

Previously

He walked down the barely lit cobblestone street, turning off into alleyways once he reached the end of the block. It was the usual way he took to get home after work. It had been one of the longest of days at work that day, for it was not usually dark outside by the time he finished and commenced his hour long journey home. Despite the long hours of dulling railway construction work, he had been feeling unsettled all day. Even as he walked now, there was a sense of dread that was present in his soul with every step.

The morning had started the same as any other. He awoke with the sun and the crowing of the roosters that surrounded the outside of the city. On the outskirts of the town, where he lived, the sound of the roosters in the morning could always be heard. It was one of the reasons he had chosen the location of his house to begin with. He knew in advanced that his life here was one that could be lived comfortably, however with much difficulty and effort on his part. The long hours that he worked every day were enough to occupy his mind to a point that kept him at a level he considered to be still relatively sane. The conditions that he worked in were, not just in his eyes, but in those of anyone who understood what he did, dreadful. He was not one that could easily have complained with any sort of justification regarding the matters of his employment, for he seemed to have been, if anything, built in a way that accepted nothing less than a life accompanied by hard labour.

Even at the peak of its place in productivity and importance, the railway was not an exclusive place that only the fittest and most resilient could call work. Many of the other men that he worked with had not the same physical capabilities as he did. In the least, he had been lucky enough to have this in his life. Known even in the part of town he lived as the strongman, the tasks of lifting railroad ties and working with other railway parts like pins were not ones that pressed stress into his life like they did into the lives of others. His stresses came from another source.

Even before his lady had awoken, he would have had left the house already to start his day. It was this small time away from her that he enjoyed every morning. It was a sense of satisfaction for him to see her sleep so soundly and peacefully. It calmed him and made his days worth something of significance. It was in these morning moments that she looked the most appealing to him, while she lay sleeping without a care or worry positioned on her visage. It was the moments in which he saw her face like this that made waking up so early in the morning worth it. With such an image in mind, work seemed only physical for his mind was always occupied by the looks and antics of his lady. Every evening he arrived home, more times than not, at an acceptable hour for dinner. In returning to his home, she would always be waiting there for him with the biggest hope of expecting him in her smile, a lovely meal that she had prepared, and all the love that living their humble lives together could have offered.

It was the simplest form of love. The love that they shared for one another was not one that could have been easily separated by the sands of time. It was original and unique. Everyone who had the pleasure of meeting them agreed upon this. There was something surreal about their relationship, something that was only able to be seen with the naked eye ever so slightly. But it was, nonetheless, there. An aspect not quite tangible, yet all the more real because of its ambiguity. It was for certain, true love. He appreciated every aspect of her well balanced character and will, and she, loved every single bit of anything that had even the slightest relevance to her man. He was, in her eyes, a work of perfection. Deserving enough of everything he might ever hope to wish for. Although the couple was by no means considered wealthy, they had something of value that could never have been measured by wealth. They had true love, and it was something that everyone throughout the city could see as clear as day. They had been blessed to have crossed paths in this life and the reactions they gave one another in their dispositions was nothing short of melodic.

The wife was a small woman, and had been her whole life. She was a native to the city, and having grown up there, a higher percentage of the population knew her by name. Her father was the practitioner on their side of the city, which was the southern part. In terms of recovery rate, he was known to have one of the highest in the city, as well as a few cities in the near vicinity. Even though it was considered as a noble trade amongst the townspeople, the father was not considered a wealthy man. He gave back most of his earnings to the city people, and left only the meagrest amounts for himself and his daughter to live off of. He did not charge anything for his services rendered except for the cost of various medical utensils if such utensils were used. A good sterile medical utensil like a scalpel was hard to find these days for any price that would have been considered reasonable by any knowledgeable practitioner. Nonetheless, he had both the richest and poorest clients within the area he practiced in, and because his intentions were known throughout the city as no less than noble, both parties were more than satisfied with paying whatever they could afford for his health services.

As far as was applicable, the husband did not fare very well with the father. He had been considered poor his whole life, and due to the fact that he grew up in a small countryside shanty with only his older sister alive to take care of him, he never really stood to understand the idea of giving any of the money one had earned back to the city. The place he grew up in deemed his family to be a bunch of invalids, and so understanding the importance of giving back to the place in which one lived was not a very conceivable idea to him at all, quite understandably so. As soon as he realized the importance of time, and living one's life, he moved away from the past, from poverty, and did everything in his power to earn an honest life and live in a way that no one else had been able to give him before.

She had been as determined as he was to live a life that would have been considered theirs in all aspects. To establish themselves as individuals within the community without having any previous precursors affecting their status amongst its inhabitants was the goal that they would come to fulfill for one another. This of course, came as much more of a task for her to complete since her father had already done so much in the community to establish their name as a reputable one; a badge of nobility that she wore also. Internally, she resented him a bit for this. There was a small part of her that wished her father had not been the one to have made the family name one of importance in the town. She had wanted to do that herself. It was an aspect of life that she held the utmost level of value to, and even in her present situation, it was a goal that she believed she might have a chance of attaining still. The uproar that did just that was caused by the couple once they had fallen in love and gotten married. To everyone, it was beyond a reasonable doubt, shocking.

The father always believed that his attempts at nobility would prove to be most beneficial to his daughter since her marrying up into the ranks of any well-known family name within the city had now become a very tangible option thanks to all of his hard work. It was not very difficult for anyone in the town to have seen the importance he held regarding her benefit and wellbeing. After his wife had died giving birth to their only child, he devoted his entire life to facilitating her success as an adult. He had wanted the best for her, but the problem that arose between the two was the fact that they did not see eye to eye in the definition of such a word as best. It was in marrying her true love, a poor immigrant fresh off the immigration boats from Ireland that she had succeeded in making her own name a recognizable one in the town. Riches or a name meant nothing to her. She wanted happiness, and simply being around him was more than pure ecstasy. Her father did not approve of the marriage; he felt as though a large slap in the face had been inflicted, and he, being a man who was not very inclined to forgiveness, did not think that he would ever be able to give her any amount of it, for it was not due in such a situation. Although, he was not one to question true love, and in every step the couple took together, side-by-side, he consistently saw in her eyes just how happy she was with her life. This he had admitted more than once to himself.

Recently, the wife had been acting strange enough for the husband to notice, and ultimately, became concerned about her wellbeing. There had been a few instances where they were having dinner and she took only to eating vegetables. The husband took concern by this only because she was not a frail girl; she had always enjoyed eating a hearty meal in welcomed company. She insisted more times than not, that her stomach had simply not been feeling too well of late, and that she believed that the nutrition in the vegetables were light enough to not upset her uneasy stomach, which could help to remedy its sickness over time. He agreed, and left the issue at that. If she was not concerned, then he really saw no reason to be concerned either. They shared a special bond, and he knew that she was not one to keeps secrets, for he was not either. They shared all aspects of their lives with each other, and functioned quite smoothly as one combined unit. The truth was yet to have been revealed, and would be only so in the latest of hours.

When he arrived home that night, she had been lying in bed, in what appeared to him at least, to be the same positioning as she had been in when he left the house that morning. It had been very late in the evening and as he walked into the kitchen and saw that she had left the dinner that she made on the kitchen table, most likely in waiting for him to arrive home, so he saw no reason to come to any other conclusion other than she had fallen asleep in waiting for him to return. He did not want to disturb her with his presence until he too was ready for bed. As long as she knew before falling into the deep slumber of the night that he had arrived home safe and content to see her sleeping so soundly after ensuring that he knew he was thought of in his absence by her preparing the lovely meal she had for him, he would rest easily that night next to her.

He sat alone at the table and began to eat the lovely meal that was in front of him. Of course he would only have enjoyed the meal itself more if she had been awake to enjoy it with him, but the current hour had not been one acceptable enough for a lady to partake in such actions. He himself enjoyed spending time alone a great deal also. Being alone with his thoughts was something that he seldom enjoyed because more often than not, it was in being alone with his thoughts that would ensure the persistence of his anxieties. The haze of confusion that would set in had always tormented him, especially the ones that surfaced during the night. Flashbacks of the past, and of the dread that he had known in his childhood, were ones that still haunted him at this time, and although they now only comprised his past, they were nonetheless aspects of his life that he would never be able to shudder. He walked with its presence on his back every morning, every night, and in every moment. His mind began to sink into its dark abysses while he ate. He looked over at his love and the commotion began to settle. She was and had always been, to him, a reminder of just how different the past had been from the present. Her presence in his life reassured him of all the good the world had to offer. As he thought of her, all of his unsettling emotions began to resolve. It was calming for him to think of how close she was, and how in a few moments, his heart would rest once more, easily. He finished eating and drinking the last sips of wine that were in his glass. Rising from the table, he pushed the chair in and put the dishes in the sink. He walked over to their bed and took off his working clothes and put on the shirt that he slept in as usual. He got into bed, and hugged his fantastic wife.

He immediately froze. His heart dropped to the framework of the ground and he began to panic. She was cold to the touch. The room had not been cold. The wood in the fireplace had been burning consistently all night and the temperature, especially in the bedroom, was quite warm and toasty. He leaned over to her, frantically and kissed her hard on the cheek. Her cheek was even colder than her body and he immediately jumped out of the bed. He picked her up and shook her gently. Screaming and sobbing now, he tried to awaken her. Still holding her in his arms, he rocked her back and forth crying. She lay there in his arms a lifeless body, still with the look of youth and innocence on her visage. There was no doubt now in his mind, that she was no longer alive or rather that her soul had left her body. He sat on the side of the bed with her in his arms for quite some time before deciding what the next steps to take were.

He lacked the ability to think now. What was he to do? The part of his life that had been worth living flashed in front of his eyes. He didn't understand the events that had just occurred. He stood up, of course still holding her lifeless corpse, and decided that it might be best to bring her to the father. He was after all, the best practitioner in the city and he would most certainly know what to do. There was no other option that he knew of. He hoped more than anything, that the father might know of some way to save her, to bring her back to life. Tears streamed down from his eyes. He never really remembered a point in his life where he was able to definitively say that he had been crying. In this moment he had an immeasurable number of tears flowing down his cheeks. A sea of misunderstood sorrow outpoured for her now. He did not understand the exact lack of life in her body; she seemed all too peaceful and content. There was not a look of sadness or discomfort on her face like there was now on his. He hoped there was something the father could do. It might have been possible that she had only been passed out. His hoping for the best of the worst possible situation seemed absurd even to his own mind. He simply could not bring himself to accept the fact that she was dead. It simply could not be possible. She was fine when he had left for work that morning. She had been alive during the day long enough to have made dinner, eat, and go back to sleep. He simply did not understand what happened. How could she have perished so easily? He knew her to have been in relatively good health, and she did not seem to have any periling sickness that would explain how suddenly she had been taken away from him. She had simply faded away over the course of a few hours at most, and he did not understand.

The walk to the father's house was not far, only about ten minutes by foot from their house. It seemed now though, to have lasted longer than an eternity. He had never made the walk before being as alone as he was now. His mind could not concentrate on one thought; it was scrambling to find any sort of answer, or fraction of consolation. Nothing could be explained. How could life had been so terribly cruel to him? Why had this happened? He looked at her once more. They had almost arrived. He saw the door of the father's house in the distance, and proceeded to start running. He screamed for him, since he must have been sleeping. It was after all, the middle of the night. He reached the steps of the house and began to pound on the door. He had only hit it a few hard times before it broke down. He had not intentionally done this; he was only trying to awaken the father as fast as possible. As a result of the door having been knocked down anyways, he picked her back up in his arms and entered the house. This whole process had not been a quiet one, and the father, most likely by the sound of the bolted wooden door hitting the floor that occurred only moments ago, started rushing down the stairs. On the way down, the husband heard him stumble in the darkness. He seemed to have recovered quickly for not long after, he heard his footsteps descending down the stairs once more. Finally he reached the bottom. He was immediately attacked by the husband who began shaking him and speaking as fast as he could, asking for a solution, anything to make her better as fast as he possibly could.

He was in this moment, quite a mess. The father on the other hand, seemed relatively calm. He had more composure than most would have had in the situation and after lighting a few candles in their holders, he proceeded to try and properly address the situation that was at hand. He had the whole situation explained to him by the husband, who spoke now only at a frantic speed. Whether or not he understood any of what the husband said, he proceeded to pace slowly over to the body of his daughter and placed his hand on her neck, looking at the clock on the mantle as he did so. There was nothing now to do, even as a practitioner. He could only confirm that she was in fact deceased.

The father couldn't tell anything new to the husband that he didn't already know. The father, who was still quite calm, explained to the husband that although this was to be considered a tragedy by all, it should come only as a surprise to him. He walked over to one of the drawers near his writing desk and pulled a small envelope out of it. The husband lay still over the body of his wife, crying and pleading with the Gods to do something, anything to change the damned life he believed to have finally escaped from in meeting her. His whole life seemed to have been followed by a sombre cloud. Truly he believed that its presence had vanished from his life when he met the woman that he would come to call the sunshine in his step. It seemed now, in the darkness of the night, that such cloud never vanished form his life, it was clear now that it had simply been preparing to rain.

Last Words

He took the envelope from the father and tucked it into his pocket. He assumed it only to have been her will or a note that was to be given to him upon her death regarding personal affects. In all honesty he did not pay much attention to it, for he could only focus now on his wife's cold body. The father told him many times that it would have been fine if he wanted to leave her overnight with him, for it would allow that he might be able to rest a bit before having go to work in the morning. Although the husband heard what the old man was saying, he did not acknowledge that he was listening. All he could think about was the suddenness of it all; he still lacked the ability to understand what had occurred. He wished it had all been a dream. He wished that instead of falling asleep that night, he would simply have woken up. It was all too surreal, and the only explanation he could think of that brought him any sort of explanation was that it was all one cruel joke being played on him by his subconscious as he slept. Surely, this could not be real. As much as he wanted this to be true, it simply was not. The sinking in off all the events that occurred that day came to be known as the most real pain he had ever felt flow through his veins and it would be a long time before he would possess the ability to forget the influx of emotion he was currently experiencing.

He had not the ability to leave her alone now either. He did not wish to leave, nor to leave her with her father in the house either. There was a part of him that simply couldn't. That night, he futilely attempted to lie down on the floor next to her cold body and tried to sleep. The father bade him goodnight and prepared his candlelight to go back up the stairs, back to his bed. There was nothing that could have been done for her at this time of night, for all the affairs that were to take place next would occur in the light hours of the day.

She rests now, in a small, unmarked grave off the countryside of the town, amongst the corpses of the rest of the town's deceased. Her burial was not a lavish one, but rather one of a more meagre classification. She had only her father and husband to attend it, which might have been even one more than she would ever have wanted to be present for such an event. There really is not much to say to the effect of her death, for within its time, nothing unusual would ever come to be said about it. It is only in the events that followed after it, after the father moved on with his everyday life, and after the husband failed to do just the same, that our interest in such a story starts to peak.

A few weeks later, the husband realized that he had completely forgotten about the piece of paper that the father had handed to him the night she died. He remembered its existence one night while he was laying in his bed trying to comprehend how it might have been possible for her to have kept such grave illness a secret from him for the remainder of her life. There was a very small whisper in his mind that made him think he might have been kept him in such ignorance as a result of her lack of love towards him. She might not have truly loved him, and this might have prompted her to feel as though she had only the option of dying alone. As he remembered the piece of paper, he got up and began to locate it. After a few minutes of frenzied searching, believing that he might have lost it, he pulled it finally out of the inner pocket of his waistcoat. He took the paper out, and examined it carefully. It appeared to be two sheets that had been hand written and folded in half to somewhat conceal their message. Before he opened it, he understood it to be her last will, so he took a deep breath, inhaling and exhaling. After he was mentally prepared to do so, he proceeded to read:

My dearest love,

It may come as no surprise to you now that your receiving this letter has only been the by-product of my cruel and untimely death. I do not have much to say to the affect of the sickness that has befallen me; father has assured me that I have no more than a few weeks of time left to live before it will take me. I can say only that this has come upon me as the greatest level of misfortune, for I have been informed that nothing can be done to slow down the sickness' grips on my body. I'd like for it to be known above all else, that my love for you will never die and shall remain immortal when I have physically long vanished into the depths of the earth.

I owe the happiness that I feel each and every day entirely to your presence in my life, and I can say that you most certainly have made me happier than I could have ever hoped to be without you in my life. It might be plausible then to say that my death, has not, at least for me, come as all too discerning of an ending. The only thing that this life seems to have deprived me of is time. It would have pleased me greatly to have spent the rest of my life with and to have grown old with you.

When I was a small child I had a dream that one day, I would awaken and I would not feel any sort of need to do anything except live. I would wake up in almost a sort of daze, completely happy and fulfilled, without a care in the world. I would have reached a point in my life where I would not mind the thoughts that others held about me, because my happiness was foremost the most important thing to fulfill. That fateful day when we met each other at the bakery, I will never forget. It seemed that I realized almost instantly the impact you were to have in my life, and the importance you would come to hold. I was taken aback by everything about you. The mystery of your past, the arrival on the coast of your future, and most of all, it beguiled me to think that above all the other choices you had made in your life, you chose me. I have, in my life, never been one to have any sort of luck, yet I consider meeting you to have been the one and only thing that has occurred in my life to make me feel as lucky as a God. Never in my wildest dreams would I ever have thought that the level of happiness I have in your presence was one that actually existed. As luck would have it, I am privileged enough to have had just that in my lifetime.

It makes me kneel over in pain to think of what might occur to your wellbeing without me in your life. I know that I have grown to be dependent on your love and presence in my life, and you the same to mine, and I cannot imagine the aching that is housed in your demeanour currently. My love I would like for it to be known simply, that I wish for you to have the ability to come to terms with my death in a reasonable fashion. Whatever may come your way, any struggle or foe, remember please that I am with you every step of the way. Physically, my presence may be absent, but in spirit, it would seem logical to think that my presence has only increased due to my passing. As unfortunate as the whole ordeal is, If I am given the option of eternally looking after you from above, then I can safely say I am not sad to die at all. The human spirit is one that we have not even scratched the surface of understanding yet.

I am not sad to die. I am sad that you must live on without me. I know certainly that if your death was the one that occurred instead of mine, that I would certainly not be able to bear the pain. I cannot imagine what emotions will fester within your soul as a result of my death. I have only, after all, known the happiness that you have given me. Please for me, try to bear the pain. Live on without me. You, my love, have always been the strongest person, and I know, that you will come to live on. Live for me, for the loss of the one whom you loved once.

I do not know if it can be labelled so easily as a last wish, but my not telling you of this illness which has fallen upon me has come only after a careful calculation of how living the rest of my life out would make me feel the most fulfilled in the end. What would making a large scene about the whole ordeal do for anybody? I'd like to think nothing at all really. It might have had negative effects if any. I tried to think logically about the whole situation. Living this wonderfully simple life with you, day after day has been the reason I feel as though I am now so capable of letting it go. Everyday seems to slip from my hands more rapidly than the last, only to be described as the most fantastic of times. Yes, it is now known now that I had been aware the whole time about my impending death, but this secret was shared only with the man who told be about the diagnosis, my father. Once he informed me of the terrible news, I initially had no response to give him. I could see the lines of misery start to crease into his face. It pained me greatly to think of everyone in pain over my illness, then mourning over my death. Why must the end of one's life result only in mourning? I am writing this now, saying completely that even though I am in agreement that my life has come to the most abrupt of unjust endings, I am not in agreement in mourning over its loss. These last years that we have spent together have been all that I have ever wanted; they have been perfect. Ultimately, I'd like to thank you for all this, for making all of my dreams come true. To think, I have so much to thank you for, so much you have given to my soul, yet the only thing that can serve as a thank you is my death. If irony did not exist I should find great difficulty in even trying to describe such a situation.

I hate my poorly constructed body for having to leave you so soon. I am not one to present negative feelings in regards to anyone, but I do feel most of the time as though I have been damned to being taken from this earth before my time. It is funny to think, even growing up I never really understood the concept of time. I guess my conflict with it may only come to continue on the next life, if such a thing existed. I know that when we were children, we did not know each other, and so there is much ignorance that cascades between you and I in its respects. I have evaded asking such questions to its relevance simply because I know partly that it was a time which you have long sought to forget. Perhaps, you also, have difficulties with the comprehension of time as it is presented to you then. Even though, I understand the ending of my own life as a tragedy, I ask you now, to please try and understand that in not informing you of it all, I was not trying to keep you in the dark, or inflict further pain. I just wanted to live the rest of my days out doing exactly what had make be so happy in the first place.

Now, there isn't really much more I can hope to say here. I have never written such an item as this before, and of course I know I never shall do the same again. It is strange sometimes to think of just how different your life can be in the changing of an hour. How I know I will miss you more than the sun misses the moon in the morning sky. While one sleeps, the other works hard, and vice versa as they switch roles in the evening. Like the very relationship they hold, my feelings for you shall remain in time as long as it progresses day after day.

Above all, please remember me. I will and have always been yours. You have forever, trapped my love. I love you without time and shall be watching over you as long as my spirit inhabits this earth. Please take care of yourself.

Death Was in the Air

He tried day after day, to live on, to carry on. He found much difficulty in this, for not even waking up was an action that he did without her in some way on a daily basis. She really had made his day every morning in looking so calm and peaceful as she slept. As they passed now, each morning seemed to sink deeper and deeper into the image he had last seen of her. The face of his dead beloved seemed to be the only one that remained in his mind now. She had looked so peaceful in that moment, so calm. He wondered about the presence of any differences on her disposition between the two states of life and death. Now that he had only his memories to serve him the answer to such questions, he vexed over the two. It was extremely unsettling for him to admit, even only on some level, that she looked more or less the same sleeping as she had when she was no longer alive. This was the most chilling fact that he would tangibly shudder to every time he tried to think of any of the differences. The fact was that there wasn't any, or at least to him there wasn't. Whether the latter or the other be the one that remains true, I think it mattered not for him, since it had always been clear that the illness of the mind that would develop as the by-product of attempting to answer it would come as a reason to change everything.

Despite all of the difficulties that came along with waking up every day, it was nonetheless an action that he did manage to successfully do every morning. Even so, it was in his actions that something was missing. He woke up, got ready, and eventually would go to work, but there was a certain element of will to do it that was lacking. He did these things without soul, for he did not want to do them; not truly at least. He was kind of just going through the motions. His attempts to want to live his life without her were ones that would never be made with any sort of success.

After a while of doing this, or going through his daily routine over and over again, it became much more clear that in all reality he did not want to live. His life simply, had been worth living at one point, and it currently was no longer. He did not want to live, he had no will to live. The pain in his mind, heart, body, and spirit simply weighed constantly on all these facets of his life. Her death now seemed to be all that was present. No will to do anything, no happiness to be found, nothing. His life now was entirely empty and faded.

One morning, just like any other, he awoke to the sounds of the roosters crowing. Instead of getting up almost instantly as he would have any other day, he simply laid there. In his bed, looking up at the ceiling, then he began to wonder about why this had all happened to him. He tried to put stark into the purpose his life might actually hold on this earth. Tragically enough, his mind remained empty. He was not able to think of anything except the fact that he had once, been able to come up with an answer to a question that never existed. The question she had answered was not one that could be easily asked by another, for it was one that did not exist. It was the question of love, of happiness, and of fulfillment. It was a question of other sorts; one that was not meant to be answered by the mind or the body. A question of the soul was its sort. She made his life worth living; she was his very own petite ray of sunshine.

This idea, this concept, was a constant in his mind. If he knew anything it was that. He knew this only now due to the fact that her presence was no longer one that was there. Like the slithering of a snake, he felt only the love that had been there all along because it was not there anymore. Not to say that he felt that he had mistreated her. No, this was not the case. He felt as though he had accepted the happiness that his life had come to be, and the good things that surfaced in his life. For as long as he could remember, his life had been only gloomy. He had only negative aspects of his childhood available for recollection.

He hated the fact that in this daze of happiness and bliss, somewhere along the line, he came to believe it. Time had brought him to believe that he actually had a chance at happiness. That everyone had equal chances in finding their own little square of happiness. Even in finding his, he had come to learn that achieving this level of ecstasy did not require much for him. He did not have much, even now. He had a small house, a wife, and a reliable job. That was the extent of his ecstasy, and that was all he required to reach such a level. Now, he had nothing. He had accepted his life as everything he had ever hoped for, and as soon as he came to believe that all the misery in his life had only been present to differentiate from how he felt when happiness had found him. He realized that the exact opposite night have been true.

As a small child he really did believe this. He believed that one day he would be happy. He would grow up to make it out of poverty, he would find someone who would love him for who he was, and everything would fall into place from there. He believed with the hope of a small child that all these things were possible. When they finally came to find a place in his life, he seemed at first unable to believe it all. And as each day went on, he began to believe in it more and more. It made him content to think that he had actually achieved his dreams. He looked back upon the small boy who believed that happiness would find him one day, and smiled that the man he was now had achieved it all. Even against all of the odds, he knew what happiness was. He had captured it after all these years. He believed in its reality.

He left his house that day in more of a broken state than the last. It seemed on this day that time had worked in a backwards fashion, for the pain and the sorrow seemed all the more settled in his soul than it had been the last few days. He walked down the cobble stone street, with his shoulders hunched over; and with lameness present in his walk, his head stayed perched to the floor of the street as he proceeded. He did not eat breakfast that day; it did not suit him. Since her death, one of the most difficult things for him had been food. She had always cooked for him and taken care of him in that regard, and so not only did he find difficulty in preparing food for himself, but he found difficulty on eating it also. He was a tall man, and after the first few days of attempting to consume food and failing, he finally came to forcing himself to eat. He really did not want to. If it had been truly his choice he would rather have stopped eating entirely, but it was imperative that he try to in the least, eat. Even if he was eating only based upon the appeasement of her wishes.

He walked down the street minding none of the others around him. Out of the corner of his eye, a neighbour had begun to approach and greet him, but he did not pay any attention to him. He was not even aware of the neighbour's presence in all honesty. He spent the entire morning more or less in the company of his mind. He was oblivious to all other around him. Even when he arrived at work, he had been distant from all the others that day.

He began his work like any other day on the railroad. This day had been a special one, for it was the day that they finished connecting the two railways that they had been working on. There had only been a few more railways to install. The men had attempted to finish it the night before, but they deemed it a better idea to complete it the next day, for it would have been much better to finish it in the light where they could admire their work for a short period of time before a train would make its way down the track for the first time. It was scheduled for noon; which allotted them approximately four hours to finish it off. Since it was a cool sunny day, the weather conditions were favourable also for the perfect ending to the journey they had long been working on. In total it had taken almost two whole years for them to build the railway from one end to the other.

Most of the other men that he worked with were considered by the townspeople as undesirable also. Some were immigrants, others visible minorities, but most had simply been born into poverty. There was a sense of accomplishment, of belonging to be found in the completion of a railway. The men all took pride in their work. After all, many a friend had died in its construction. It was the privilege of the foreman to have slipped the last railroad tie into its place on the track. A few other workers then bolted it down to secure its place. The railway was finally complete. Everyone stepped back and gazed at their magnificent piece of work. It was truly something to be proud of.

He stood amongst the other men, and tried to find the emotions that the other men were displaying on their faces now. Pride, happiness, and fulfillment. They all felt it. They all wore it. He had even managed to muster up a smile for the railway. It was after all, something that he had quite a large part in building. It was something to be proud of. He knew that the emotion which he was now wearing on his face was one that did not surface naturally from his mind. He smiled absently. His mind focused still only on the darkness, and on the shadows. Underneath his smile, he was more than distraught that he had been a part of finishing something so great, and now had no one to share it with.

There came a sound in the distance, and in one instantaneous motion, all heads were turned towards it. All of the workers became overjoyed with the sound of the train as it started coming within sight of the left hand corner of their eyes. It was still some distance off, but the honks that the train made were definitely now distinguishable. He too motioned his head toward the noise. For the first time in a while, he caught himself smiling if his own will once more. He was happy to see the train coming on the track that was for certain. The smile that had bloomed out of the shadows slowly crept up to completion. He took the deepest breath. He had also come to realize too now that this was indeed an occasion meriting happiness. Everyone looked at the train as it crept faster and faster into a carved image from the coloured blur it had been just moments ago. Everyone began to clap and the train began to come into plain view. He too clapped along.

As he looked at the train, it seemed now that his smile had been completely wiped away from his face, although there was still a whisper of satisfaction in it. He took another beep breath, this time with his eyes closed. He let out all the breath in one accepting decompression. He opened his eyes and looked at the train now not far off from where he stood. He began pushing his comrades aside as he walked forward, trying to get a closer view of the train. Once he was almost in front of the track, the train was about to pass by the group of men. The others were cheering and waving to the passengers that were in the train as they passed. As he took one last breath, he walked into the center of the track. As the train came to pass the group of men, it also came to impale him on the front grill. All life faded from his body, and he laid on the other side of the track where the train had thrown him. He had the same look of calmness, peace, and serenity expressed on his face now.

His bloodied and lifeless body lay on the track, as others around began to realize what had just happened. Most had not even paid attention to him before the incident. They had not even realized that he decided to take his own life that day until the train had passed them entirely, where they then saw the mangled body that remained on the track. He was so close to the tracks, so close to it all, that no one even realized what he had planned to do. Once everyone knew what had occurred, and they called upon the foreman to clean up the mess his body had made on the new track. No one really paid too much attention to his death other than the foreman, who had to in order to clean the track and find any sort of family or relative that might want to claim the body. Slowly, the men filed out of the area, after all, their work had been completed for quite some time now, and if they had any chance at earning a living through railway construction, they had to find another location that would employ them as soon as possible. Some might even take their time in doing anything, choosing to spend the rest of their day off at the pub with spirits and friends. The foreman, for the time being, remained back from the group and proceeded to go up the track to where the body was. He looked at it for a moment in shame and dishonour for he knew that the man had taken his own life. The foreman had only spoken to him a few times, and from those times, did not know if he had any kin or family members to bring the body to. The foreman couldn't help himself but notice the look of serenity on his face also. He stood there looking at him for quite some time, entirely perplexed at the face that would remain displayed until the body began to decompose and become one again, with the soil.

The foreman then picked up the body and brought it over to the bin where all of the excess pieces of rock bed and cleared away material were placed. Although it was difficult for a man of his smaller stature to complete such a task, he succeeded in hiking the man up over his shoulders and into the waste bin. He had no family, he was not important, so this is where his body was to decompose.

The man who took his life for the love of another never came to have a proper burial. It is said now, that sometimes in the middle of the railway, at the very place where he committed the deed, a welcoming figure has been seen by the conductors that have come to pass it. The few times that this has happened, nothing bad has ever occurred either before or after the event, but every time he appears to be seen, it is only in the moments that are too late for the train to ever stop.

Perspectives of Death

I must say that it was, more than a relief to see him sleeping so peacefully every night. The day seemed to drag on and wear away the tone of calm that he wore on his face when he woke up in the morning. Every night when the sun started to rise in the night sky, I knew it was almost time for him to wake up. The grief would soon set into him and I would feel the most intense feeling of guilt and helplessness once more. I hated seeing him like this, even more so knowing that there was absolutely nothing I could do to heal the situation. I was simply there, a stagnant figure. There is nothing worse than seeing the level of pain that you might have caused in the person you love. I am not sure about the time that had passed thus far, but I am certain that it has been at least a few months. I have still not adjusted to his constant level of pain. Every day I experience the same levels of these feelings with him. As of yet they have not diminished at all, which has now come raise a level of concern within me. I can feel now that something is wrong. I believed that it might simply have been the result of my death, but I dread that something else has surfaced. I cannot explain exactly what sort of feeling it is, but it is one that I am most certainly concerned about. It is not exactly a feeling of dread but perhaps one of a foreboding nature. The uncertainty of the feeling itself concerns me also.

I sensed as soon as he woke up that something had been different this day. He woke up as he usually did, however instead of getting ready to take on the day, he remained in bed for quite some time, staring at the ceiling. As I looked down upon him, I wondered if he could see me, or even if he sensed that I might have been there. This was after all the first time our eyes might have had the chance at meeting since my death. He looked straight up at the ceiling, simply staring. As much as I wished he had the ability to see me, I knew this to be only an absurd idea. After all, even if he had seen me, or even if he just knew that I was there; such notions would only lead to a festering idea within him. He would not be able to tell anyone, for even I must admit, would dismiss such idea as folly and suggest he take a trip to the local sanatorium. Nonetheless, he stared in my direction for quite some time before he decided to proceed on with his day. All I could do was the same. Even now, looking at him, he was still the most fantastic being I had ever met. Even though I was the only person to have ever seen it, I always thought him to have held himself with an air of nobility.

It was little facts like this, little things that only I saw in him, that made me feel the most comforted. I knew that if it was only I that could see these things, it might deter the chances of losing him to another. A large fear of mine had always been just that. As I look at him now, I can conclude that such ideas surely were the by-product of anxiety, but when I was alive I believed truly that someone would come into his life one day, and he would fancy them over me. That is, for me, one of the hardest facts to admit. It was only in the end that I believed with all my heart that he loved only me. I feel ashamed to say, that up until that point in my life, his presence seemed too fantastical to be true. This was something I really could never explain. I understood it as love, but I understand it now as something else. I watch over him now for a reason that I am certain is not just love. It is clear now, that another sort of connection exists between him and I.

As the day began to set in his face, so did the pain begin to set in my heart. The feelings that ran through my being now were ones that came with the most difficulty to describe, for I identify them now as a figure that exists only within the eyes of death.

Today was the day that the workers were set up to finish the railway they had been working on for the past two years. It was an exciting day for all of them, and as we came to stand next to them, the excitement could easily be seen on all of their faces. Personally, I too was excited. I never really left the house when I was alive, and it certainly was thrilling to see something as new and revolutionary as a train. It made me especially happy to see this one knowing that it was an end that my love had been a part of creating. However, he had not the same expression of joy on his face as I did. He remained still, and as depressed as he had been for the past months. I wished he would, even if it was simply for a moment, smile at the accomplishment that he had been a part of completing To build the track for a train that would connect one side of the country to another was one of the most extraordinary things that one could say they had a hand in accomplishing.

One of the strange facts about my current composition is that I cannot hear sounds. I find it strange that as a soul on the earth that does not have a body to house itself, I have none of the senses at my disposal except sight. I cannot touch, I cannot hear, I cannot speak, and I cannot taste; yet I have the ability to see. I am certain that since this is the only sense that I have retained as a soul, there is something else that this must mean and I have yet to figure it out. At the current moment the only relevancy such a fact bears is to describe the fact that I could not hear the train as it approached the track. As the heads of the workers turned to meet the surfacing shades of the train in the distance, I took notice of this, and turned my head to meet it also.

It was interesting to see the colours appear out of the distance, and after a few seconds, the outline of the train was completely visible. As everybody else started clapping and cheering, I also felt the urge to do so. I was cheering for the train. Body or not, it was still quite an exciting thing to see. My love started to catch the excitement bug also. As a result of this I dedicated a small smile to him. This was the first time he had smiled since my death. It made me incredibly happy to see that smile I had come to hang onto so strongly, I was beginning to think the possibility of me existing in this state and never seeing him smile again was inevitable. I understand completely that he is sad, for I hated seeing him like this also, perhaps even more so due to the fact that I knew only my death as being the cause for this immeasurable amount of sorrow.

The train was much closer now, and the newly painted vibrant green on its sides seemed to glimmer in the sunlight. I had an immaculate view of the train. It bewildered me somewhat, to think that such a new and great technology existed in this time, and I was blessed enough to have seen it, even if sight was my only conception of it. As excited I was, I took a break from train gazing and looked back upon my love. This action was only prompted by the feeling that I had when the day started. It had gone away, for quite some time, but usually as these things do, it sparked inside my being once more in this moment.

His eyes were closed now, and on his face he displayed only the most calming of looks. He looked without worry, without care. At peace I would say to an extent. He took a deep breath and as he expelled the warm and dry air that filled his lungs he placed his arms out by his sides and looked up. It seemed strange to me to notice that no one else felt the urge to pay any attention to his actions since it was all I had the ability to focus on. As the train came to pass, the excitement felt by others, I could tell, was much more intense than it had been minutes ago. Taking a deep breath that expanded his chest, he began to walk toward the train.

No, my love please don't. I realized now, what he sought out to attempt. My love, I cannot tell you more in this moment than any other, please do not do this. I value your life more than I valued my own. I am here now watching over you; with the intensions of ensuring your safety and wellbeing, not this. Not this, never this. My love, I believe you have failed to realize that there was nothing that could have been done about my death, it was imminent from the start. I wanted you to be happy, to in the least, attempt to live on this earth the best you could without me. I swooped in front of him, in front of the train and started to scream and plead him to change his mind. Of course, my cries were not heard. I tried to push him back, to push him away. My arms went right through him, as I knew they would. My cries were not heard, for they did not exist. No tears flowed form my eyes, for all they could do was bear witness.

The train came to pass; its center impaled him and he lay there now on the track, a completely mangled and disfigured corpse. Like a small helpless child, my presence stood still now. I looked upon his body and I could only stare. My love, what have you done? It was in this moment that I realized I did not understand. My mind raced. I tried with every ounce of power I had to understand why he believed this to be the only option. My love, I wished never for you to do this. My love, I feel now as the only one to blame for the taking of your life. My form allowed me to exist on this earth as a protector, and I failed to do even this. I failed in the one task that I had as a soul. Worst of all, it was you my love, my soul mate, whom I failed to protect.

Almost instantly, I felt something else. As I stared at this lifeless body, it became apparent that his soul had started to escape it. He rose up into the sky. His eyes met mine, and in that moment, I forgot all of the sorrow I had just come to know. It was in this form, in this way, that made it possible for him to see me now too. I wiped the emotions off my face and went towards him with open arms. I never thought for a moment about the present one. He too smiled the truest of smiles in seeing me, and rushed toward me also with open arms. In ending his own life, he gave up his physical body, which allowed him to be only a soul, as I was now. All my pain, all my sorrow, and all the hate that I developed for myself these past few months as a soul simply vanished. It was the most overwhelming feeling in this entire universe; to be reunited with the one and only person you have ever loved. We had not the ability to speak any words to each other; we had only the ability to love each other in this moment. As he hugged me, and I him, the world stopped. I could have stayed in this place now, in the overbearing comfort of his arms forever. Even when I was alive, I don't believe I had ever experienced such an influx of emotion. It is hard to describe the level of happiness that was in both of our souls now. Gladly enough, I cannot offer a third party birds eye view of it at all. I can say however, that it was the most perfect of moments. I loved this man, and he I. There was nothing more that mattered.

It seemed our reunion lasted only a few short moments before it vanished into thin air, leading ultimately to the meaning of my existence now in its totality. I would like for it to be clear firstly, that one cannot take such a moment of fulfillment away without consequence. My world in its entirety, in hugging my love again since my death, was perfect. The only thing I had wanted in the afterlife, the only thing I sought ever was to see him one last time, to have the possibility of actually saying goodbye to him, for that was something I had not done in person. As quickly as I had been welcomed into his arms, was a quick as he was ripped away from mine. I felt it. He felt it. There was nothing that could be done. It was not a force of this world I believe. It came from somewhere else, from underneath us. Now, as an external force ripped us apart, we tried with every ounce of our strength to stay connected. I am certain the universe could hear me cry. Whatever it was, it wanted only him. I felt no force upon me, only him. If it was us they wanted, no such problem would have ever existed. Gladly we would have went anywhere, as long as we were together. I felt him slipping away. His arms taken away from my back, my head away from his chest, my arms away from his waist, and his head away from mine. In one instant it was all gone.

He vanished into the ground underneath me. This moment in time I will never forget. How could I possibly ever? It is this moment that the grips of time has been unable to take away from me. My soul cannot forget. It will not forget; it does not want to forget. For, if ever there was a man, who deserved to be in the favour of time, it was certainly him. My love, as I understand it, your soul became entangled with the direst of fates when you decided to jump in front of that train. I believe your being ripped away from me to be the by-product of a contract that has long existed between the world and the one that has come to be known to us as the Devil. My dearest love, even though I understand your reasoning for such actions now, telling you that he owns your soul comes as the most regretful news that I have ever had to deliver.

However my love, I understand the events as this also. All hope is not lost. These lives, I am certain of it, would never have offered you to me in either form, if I had not a part to play in this. As I have said before, a part of my soul is linked to yours, and shall be forever. It is this part of me, this love that I have and will always have for you, that shall allow us to be reunited finally once more. Please, I understand that the place you are right now is not the ray of sunshine you had come to know as life when it was lived with me, but you must understand that the task I have been given is not an easy one. My love, I am certain of it, that if I can prove our love is strong enough to exist without the confinements of time, then I am certain your soul shall be returned to this earth, to me and to you. The simple fact of the matter remains that, your soul was not ever the Devil's to take. It was mine. It is mine, and shall be mine until the end of time.

Concerning the Devil

I speak now only to the effect of the Devil. I wish to settle this matter in the most reasonable of methods. There is no need to get out of hand here. In all due politeness to you, I'd like to make it very clear that I do not wish to quarrel with you or attempt to degrade your name in any way. Please believe me when I say that even in my darkest of dreams I would never try to associate myself with you; I understand the grave dangers involved with executing such a task. However, I hope in the least that you can come to understand exactly the situation that I am currently in. I am not accusing you of making a mistake, nor am I accusing you of taking something wrongly from me. The simple fact of the matter is that my soul mate did kill himself, and because of such actions, was damned to spend eternity in Hell with you. In the sea of souls that exist under your claim; I believe the one that is in question here should not mean all that much in terms of numbers. I can imagine the question of a claim on a soul to be one that could cause only moral and status conflicts. And so to begin with, I wish to address those two issues.

Firstly, let us concern ourselves with the matter of the moral conflicts that I feel could surface in your mind concerning such affairs. Yes, it is quite clear to me, that you are the Devil. I am aware that you represent all evil and sin not only in this world, but perhaps in others too. I am aware that you own the underworld, and that you deal only in the processing of souls. This is to say that you as a being of business stand to per se tarnish your name in releasing a soul from the underworld. Please understand that I can understand such ideas. Even the Devil must uphold a certain moral code, even if he is to say, evil. Apparently, the rules dictate that any one person, who chooses to take their own life, shall spend the rest of their existence with you in Hell. A fact I am completely willing to accept if it were not for the catalyst that I remain to be. Fair is fair my dear. I am agreeing that you most certainly did acquire the soul of my soul mate under valid pretences, but the contract you hold with it is not under those same pretences. The affair at hand here is not at all that black and white.

The fact of the matter remains that his taking his own life was the by-product of my death. If it is not wrong enough to punish someone for not being able to bear the death of the only person they love, then perhaps a more logical approach should be presented to you. I was there, when he died, I was present and saw the whole thing as a soul. I was there too, when you decided to rip him into the depths of Hell, from which I was forbidden from following of course. It is possible to say that this might never even have been an issue if I too was permitted to spend the rest of my time as a soul with him there, with you, in Hell. Fantastically enough, I was not given such an option. I did not take my own life, nor did I live one that considered me a sinner when my body no longer served me. Having said that, since Hell was not given to me as an option, it is here that our moral conflict begins.

When my love was deemed to have lived a life unworthy of staying with me as a soul on earth, and was ripped right out of my arms; I know not whether you knew that I was in fact there. As it has come to be understood, you rule and reside in the underworld. When deemed unfit to live on, any soul in question simply floats into your midst. The rate in which this occurs I imagine, on a worldly scale, would be quite the large task for one being to complete entirely by themselves. Surely, you do not have the time to oversee each and every judgment of available souls. Of this I am certain because if such a truth existed only in opposition to such a conclusion, then I might be inclined to say that your time does not hold much value then. If you do concern yourself with every soul, with everyone, then no one is special because on a regular basis it is what you do. If your regular work day is to judge and acquire souls, then I would conclude that there is nothing really special that you do with your time; there is nothing that you can say you alone have done uniquely with your time. Certainly, a character as universally known and omnipotent as yourself cannot be the one to execute such medial tasks on a daily basis. Morally, I should think that the two simply do not match up with each other. As much as I wished that you had seen the whole event, I believe you did not. Since the latter is true, it is clear that the purpose here becomes not a question of morality, but of ignorance.

Now having said that, I do not believe you were even present when this whole situation that I am concerning myself with now occurred. So, please allow me to inform you about it all so we can address it from the same departure point. About three months prior to this incident, it was my life that was in question. I died in the comfort of my own home at the hand of a disease that would only come to be understood much later in time. These things happen, naturally, of course. It was made clear to me from the beginning that it was an illness I was not to survive. Within a few weeks, my life had come to feel complete, and so in death, I wished only that my love learn to live without me, for I knew if the roles were reversed within the same situation, I would not have been able to live without him.

When death knocked on my doorstep and crept in slowly beneath the cracks and the comfort of my bed, I was not judged based on any decision that I made in my life. It was the strangest occurrence to be able to say that I have truly experienced. I do not remember much about the transition period that took place after my death, but I do remember the moment in time where I took notice of myself, and saw that I was not housed within a body anymore. I was simply present. I was there in my home, but not really. Not physically, not tangibly. I call this experience strange because I was the only one that as far as I could see, was in such a state. I went with my love to work every day, and it struck me odd that I did not see anyone else that had the same composition as I did, even more so considering I had only one of the senses at my disposal, that sense being the one of sight. Why was I the only one that got to accompany a living person? Was it just me, or did I simply not have the capability to see other spirits?

In complete honesty, I would much enjoy having the answers to such question, but as far as you are concerned in this matter, the answers are not relevant. The relevancy that I am hoping to have established here is the point that in death, I did not rise to the heavens, nor did I get plunged into the depths of Hell. I simply stayed where I was and was given the opportunity to protect the man I loved, which was, even considering the shortcomings of the situation, fantastic.

Clearly then, my presence on earth would not even have occurred, if it served not a purpose. This I knew even as a soul. I cannot say however, that I did ever come to a conclusion about what that purpose was. I assumed that it was to protect my love and to watch over him, since that was the first thing that I felt like I had already been doing. It was instinctual almost. I never thought the point would come where my presence as a soul would serve as a witness for the one event that had tragically come to shape and define me in time. That's simply it. I'd like for it to be very clear that you have not only wrongly acquired his soul, but you have also a piece of mine. And that is a fact that furthers the case I am trying to make here. I think that because I was present when he killed himself, a part of my soul was also ripped away with him. Now yes, I understand that the validity of my vision is in question since we may not ask such a question validly if there were others present also. Well the answer here lies in the fact that I witnessed it as a soul. I witnessed the event as a soul and yes, I did have a personal connection with him, so when he assumed the form of only a soul as I was too, he saw me. I'm sure he was not surprised to see me there, but then I am prompted to ask also, if he knew he would see me once his soul passed on, why would he take his own life knowing the repercussions that would follow? The hardest thing I have ever been somewhat forced to do was witness the one person that I had hoped to protect from death and from harm, kill himself.

To be witness to such an event, please try to imagine for a moment, is shocking enough. But when, the being whom the event is happening to is the man that you loved your entire life and watched over your entire after life, there is no possibility that I can simply ignore being witness to such an event and continue to live on. No this affair needs to be settled, and it needs to be settled now.

Secondly, we must address the issues of status. I am not going to praise you, or call you almighty, or powerful. You are everything that is evil in this world, and I shall not pander to such follies. I will however, address the issue of status that arises in the returning of a soul. You may be concerned now, that your status as the Devil might tarnish if it becomes known that you are returning a soul. The retuning of a soul might skew the judgment of others to believe that you have lost some of what every soul has come to fear. Let me assure you that we are going to address this now. This situation is the exception to the rule. The exception comes from the involvement of souls in the affair. If it was simply between yourself and him, the story would be different. But, since I have also been intertwined in this, I would dare say, maybe even more so than the man whose soul is in question, your status should not suffer. We are all mature here, and this issue can indeed be solved without anyone's status or morals suffering damage. In quite the opposing effect, I believe that in its remaining stagnant, such an affair might damage more than just one status or morality, since it has already come to define my existence.

It is here that you shall see your contract come to be voided. You see the duality of this whole situation has only come to occur based on the fact that my soul too has not the ability to move on either. I am here on Earth living, in a perpetual loop, unable to move onto the next stage of life. I am stuck on this one event, of course, as anyone sane person would be. One life to the next, I have only the option of trying to get his soul back for him. Life after life, I am doomed to live without the hope of moving onto something different, even if the something different was something as simple as living for a different purpose. Your contract is void here, because in taking his soul, you have also marked the course for my soul. His soul affects mine, and I have made it clear from the start that I wish not ever to willingly enter into business with you, for you are the Devil and in the least, I am a desirable target for you. The dangers that have come along with attempting to retrieve his soul are ones that do frighten me beyond belief, but alas for my love, they are worth it. Ultimately, it is worth it for me also. I deserve to have the option of life after death. I deserve to be a free soul with a choice. I shouldn't have to live life after life in constant darkness, hoping, wishing, that one day I will be complete once more having found happiness and ultimate fulfillment.

Do you understand now? You cannot have his soul. I hate to be so robust, but I am not really giving you much of an option here. As clearly as I see it, his soul does not belong to you. My presence on this earth serves as enough proof for such a fact. I would not be a living presence here if it did, for I would have moved on to the next world long ago. Yet, I have not the ability to do so yet. And that, my dear is a clear violation of a soul's rights', nullifying the contract that you hold with my love. Simply put, I own his soul, you do not.

The Immortality of the Soul

My presence in this periodization of time has not come to me as one that I have found to be of a leisurely or gratified nature. It is one however, in which I have come to question the possibility that one's soul might have the ability to move through time in a way which when embodied in the form of a human, or any other living thing, are not able to do so. To say this in terms that are easier to grasp, I am to say that it is in using our souls that allow for us to travel through time. I mean to expand on the immortality of the soul in saying this, not the actual physical idea of a human being able to travel through time or space, for as I have made it very clear already, that is a completely absurd notion.

Indeed I understand just how difficult of a task it is to try and understand and expand upon a subject, that we as an entire human race have yet to put any sort of concrete understanding into. We know nothing really about the soul, other than the fact that it is a notion that humans have had ideas about since the beginning of time, or rather conceptual history, it seems. The volatility of time comes to intercept the truth to be had about such subjects also, since it progresses along a forwarding line, it seems that our notions and conceptions of such ideas have also come to do just that. With the aim of helping to establish some sort of universal standard or conception about the soul I have only my personal experience to offer.

My expansion on this subject occurred only in thinking about the effects that Vergil had on me and my feelings in this life. I mean to say that even though the events have come to differ extremely with the evolution of time, the feelings that I felt in the past life that we spent together and the current life in which we lived in now, were one and the same. The journey had been different, but the conclusion that I came to arrive at was the same as it was in the last life. I felt as though I had let him down, as though it was somewhat my fault that we couldn't be together; the same feelings that I had at the end of the first life after he chose to kill himself. I felt the same on the inside as I had the last time. Knowing that I had never felt like this before, that I had never had any sort of tangible explanation to associate with these reoccurring feelings, I understood it to be something different. It seemed to me that the immortality of one's soul was something that might come to be understood within this whole affair.

To help further explain allow me to present the example in question here, and hopefully you will understand the specifics as I have understood them. I believe that my soul was only given the opportunity to embody living human tissue in this life because of events that occurred in a past life, with the intentions of repairing the wrongs that occurred within the events in question of course. We have all come to know that the events I have come to question remain as the presence that a man by the name of Vergil held in my life, and how I have come to feel the way I do in my current everyday life having met him, now for the second time. I know that I have met him before, for I know of him only as a man who had not a soul. The half of my soul that remains struck by the life we lived together last has come to confirm this. Without a doubt I am certain that this man is the one that is supposed to have the other half of my soul, which is also known as his soul. However, since that half was taken away from him through a technicality that has the possibility of being appealed, it is within this possibility that my mission lies.

Not to say that my soul has come from another period in time to execute such tasks, but rather that it is without a doubt stuck in the time where it bore witness to the death of it's soul mate, and the collection of its soul by the Devil that occurred in a past life. It was the trauma of this event, the cruelty of it all in relevance to my existence on this earth today that has led me to question the possibility that my soul originated in another time, and is dedicated within this time, to fulfill the task that brutally altered it in the last life. That is what I mean to say about the concept of the immortality of the soul and its ability to travel through time.

I believe that the Devil was not aware of the fact that this soul in question was predetermined to have had a mate by which the sheer acknowledgement of the others existence would lead to ultimately seeking to end the terms of contract that were established in its absence. My reasoning for conflict lies solely with the Devil. My life has, up until now, been filled only with sadness, sorrow and hardship. With Vergil, I felt truly happy for the first time. Not only for a few moments but for the longest period of time I have ever felt happiness for also. I can understand that to lose one's soul to the Devil in exchange for what I have considered in this life to be eternal perfection in the way that Vergil presented it to me, is an action that may seem desirable. To have the ability to evade the tyranny of beauty, to be the visage of perfection. I use such a description now only because I truly do believe in this life that the lack of soul that I saw in Vergil was one that only I have come to find desirable. Not to say that others were not ever attracted to him, for the exact opposite was in fact true, but rather that the perfection I saw in him was grossly due to the fact that he didn't have a soul, and lives without one today. If anything, I wished that I had not the ability to see that he lived in such a condition, for it reflected my condition also. It pains me to admit that I live now as only one half of a complete puzzle piece is something that I bow my head to; I feel ashamed to say that I have yet to succeed in the completion of my soul. It is very difficult to say, whether or not the life I live currently is the first opportunity I have been given to retrieve his soul, or rather the first time I have agreed to the conditions that have lined up for me to allow do so.

However, if the consideration of having lost one's soul was the by-product of the termination of a love that was supposed to unite two souls into one, into completion, then it might be possible for the loss of the soul to not have been the ending but rather the beginning or an intermittent curve. If Vergil lost his soul in the termination of a past life in order for the chance to be with the one he loved, even if it was only for a moment, it would still mean that once the next life came around, the match to the soul might have a chance to retrieve it, if they were solely convicted to do so. It is in this respect that the relevance to the immortality of the soul comes into play.

To lose ones soul over the chance of finding true love is something that I'd like to believe at least, is worth considering. As sad as the story comes, it was in the past life that Vergil came to lose his soul. If the roles were reversed, if I had taken my own life as a result of his death, the conditions to retrieve my soul might never have surfaced in time. As I have always been, I am committed to such a cause. I am positive that true love is something that everyone can in fact universally agree on; that it is something of quite significant worth, if not the object which is worth the most to us as humans, for it is also the object that has come to bear the least amount of understanding in the passing of time.

For whatever reason, the timing was not right for our love to have fallen into place. I am committed to the idea that this expression will make a convincing enough of a case for the soul in question to be released from its eternal clasp. If it did not work in the past life between Vergil and I, it might be because it was in this life that it was meant to do so. As a woman, I would not have had the right to have expressed any sort of feelings pertaining to the subject matter expressed prior to this time period. It would have been considered witchcraft or simply an absurd notion. I would have been labelled as a recluse, a freak, no matter what catalysts present that that might have proved otherwise. It is in the passing of time, the proceeding onward in ones soul's life that I believe to be the catalyst that will set this love story to end. If not in this life, which I did indeed dread is a conclusion that can already be made, then the next one.

To wait for eternal happiness is one of the noblest things one can wait for. If one's true love has been met before the selling of either party's soul had occurred, then the soul in question would have to be refunded once the other half of the soul realized that it was not present. It was essentially cheating someone out of a soul. Even though the Devil is the epitome of all evil, even he must obey the rules. He must refund Vergil his soul and hope that it has not occurred too late and that even though true love nullified the contract, that it did not affect the terms of agreement. We may fall many times; we may get up always once more, but for some this task seems much harder to do than for others. To stay in regret for the existence of one's life does not seem impossible. And surely I believe that living an entire life without one's soul might greatly hinder the results of the souls return. The great thing about finding one's true love and one's soul mate is simply, that even though I understand that the return of Vergil's soul may or may not result in the ending I am hoping for, I really do not care. His soul must be returned to him, because it needs to prepare for the next life. I understand that giving back one's soul after a deal has already been made might give the character returning it a reflection of weakness in the eyes of onlookers. This is absurd because the contract should never have existed to begin with. It is no one's fault. In ignorance one side committed an action where the repercussions that included their soul were not thought of, for they thought only about the hope of finally being a desirable match for the soul he so longed to be with after her death.

The side of the Devil should not receive any ill-will either because he was unknowing about the facts surrounding the soul to begin with. The soul was promised to me first; therefore it was not at liberty for him to even lose. Now that I have connected with the other half I find it imperative that you return his soul to its rightful owner, because the fact remains that nowhere in the contract did it mention altering the state of anyone else's soul other than Vergil's. In losing his soul, he has greatly affected me in this present life, and my soul is eternally damaged. It is eternally half of a whole. Even though your contract may hold with him, it does not pertain to how it affects me. The soul was never yours to have and you must return it once I have proved to you that I am in fact the embodiment of the other half of soul that belongs with that of Vergil's. In making this argument and completing everything I have to say about the subject, you will understand and agree that I was the catalyst no one saw coming.

If not in this life, then in the next. I do understand the implications, if any, that the soul cannot be rejoined with its body while the body in question is still functioning without a soul. To do that to one's soul would cause even further damage because the change from the eternal brimstones of Hell to life is too severe. However, once the life in question has passed and the soul that was supposed to embody the person no longer exists as a possible connection, then the soul must be returned to the next life that it was supposed to live. I can wait until the next life in knowing that it would lead to eternal happiness in the end.

Personally, I do not believe I would mind if it was more than a few tries before completing the task in order to gain a more in depth idea of what it would mean to have actually accomplished it. To be exact, that it was necessary to make a few mistakes in order to gain more depth of feeling in its completion. As though it would mean something simply in that it was a task that you had failed at more than a few times, therefore when you would actually succeed, the success would be more appreciated. As though you can identify true success only by understanding what it meant to I find a means to achieve the ending that would end in eternal happiness. This is what I hoped to achieve. However something I did not calculate in this was the fact that I have always understood, even today. From all of the different factors in my life that speak to me, this factor was that I was not meant to live this life in happiness. This life was simply to be the precursor to happiness. A period spent fixing the mistakes of the past.

The Element of Time

Souls can only handle so much passing of time before they start to realize that time is tangible and can be measured. I set out on this journey because a feeling deep down inside of me needed to prove that time could be measured, that it was be tangible. I'd like to provide the of example death. I use only it as an example because like time, it is something that holds very little understanding within the world. Something as final as death might come as the only reasoning found in trying to explain why someone was not able to complete any certain task that they have found to be imperative of completing. If the settings to the life that occurred after the one where the task in question was never finished arise favourably again, then it would be essential to have a repetition in time and the soul might have the opportunity to finally complete it. In a way, even if time had advanced the soul would not have been able to, it is in the time which the soul is trapped that comes to define the person hosting it in the next life. It is here that the element of time and the questions surrounding it have come to my attention.

What was there to find within the conception of time? Of course there is something to be found in time, even if we as humans have not come to understand it completely yet. With regard to its relation to us, I believe there is much that we do not understand about this fourth dimension. It is interesting to think that humans are the only species on this earth that keep track of time; we are essentially, its creator. Well, surrounding the concept of keeping it on an hourly clock at least. The earth itself seems to follow a natural order with the rising of the sun and the setting of the moon every day. Now whether this can be labelled in a state of nature as time is something I cannot come to any conclusion on, for we know only time as humans and not as the universe.

However, when glancing from a distant lens one can clearly see that there is much more to the larger picture of time than we might think. As time has passed, century to century, the human race has begun to understand the importance of preserving the past, and learning what we can from it. A reflection of the time in which we live in is the example of the museum which is a location that is specifically dedicated to the preservation of the past and important events in history. The history that is then chosen to be remembered in such a way is the history that we are choosing to remember. Not only this, but the history that we do choose to remember is also in itself a reflection of the generation that chooses to value one aspect of the past rather than others. Because we decide what is important, we paint the present with the past. It is when these two intertwine that one can come to the true realization of just how time might possibly work. For example, art is if anything, solely a human creation. Because it, along with time, are two ideas that were solely created and followed by humans, they may serve as a perfect match for comparison.

Art is but a tangible fragment of time. It is in art that one sees not only the expression of the artist, but also the time that inspired and facilitated the creation of their work. It serves also as a reflection of the audience to which it is presented to, since it is also the conclusions that the audience comes to about it that come to formulate the present. A piece of art captures the tone of a mind, body, soul, time, and spirit. It is something so real, so tangible. So much can be taken from a true masterpiece. If nothing is taken away, then it reflects also the time in which the art has been presented to and perhaps the differences between the two. Centuries before the present time, art had taken on a revolution, an age of romance. As the colour palettes used became softer and more expressive, so did the stories that they told. And just as that age passed, so did the many different artists responsible for it. One classification of time flowed into the other and the art that inspired an era lead to another, and so on. It is in these reactions that a sort of story began to form. Like time, art has been around since the beginning, together forever, as two things that in the presence of one another have come to shape us as a human race.

Another example that I'd like to use solely for within the purposes of this novel is the use of language. I am inclined to write these words in a style that does not match the writing style of any other voice in this generation. The story I have told, and am continuing to tell has been done so in a manner that seems, to me at least, as being somewhat from a times past.

The only other option that might account for the difference of style I have presented is that it is the speech of the future, but certainly that would prove that time travel was possible, within the extent that the soul can allow. It would make me more comfortable to simply mean that for the sake of proving the point that one's soul might have the ability to draw on the past the valid one here. For I wish not to indulge any further into the notion of humans possibly having the ability to travel into the future. That is simply a topic that I believe should never be discussed, I would say, in any time, place, or space. Not to say that I am dismissing it as an idea, because it could certainly be possible, but I do not wish to provide any evidence to its validity, for its validity has the power to change the existence of humanity as we know it.

If ever, the human race developed the ability to time travel, I'd like to believe at least, that no such leap would ever have the ability to surface without leaving its traces in history. If time travel had already been possible, then surely there would be proof of it. It would come as no secret to the time period that developed it, that covering up the travels to the past would be imperative. There would be no scenario, I can imagine, as such a scenario where one would alter the past so severely to the extent that the future in which the time traveling device would be built would seized to have existed. Therefore, using that as a basis, I believe that fundamentally, humans have not mastered this art yet. It could very well be possible, but if ever it was, it might not be at the same time that its creator recognized the power it held.

There are many different examples of the power that time holds. In its passing, everything changes. It is the single thing in this universe that progresses forward no matter what other factors come into play. And yet, it confuses me that time is also, one of the concepts that we have not come to understand, well, really at all. We know it passes, but we cannot say much more about it. With quantum leaps in science and physics, humans have come to learn so much about the world around them and about themselves. Yet, not many leaps have been made in the understanding of time. If time, in its entirety, is simply a concept that is not meant to be understood by humans, then that must mean that it is something else. Time has, since its beginning, eluded all humans, even currently. It seems silly to think, however, the fact is that we know more about God or the notion of a God or Devil existing than we do about time. This must mean something. I personally, cannot come to any non-volatile conclusion about what that might possibly mean, but I can say that I do believe whatever it is, humans, myself included, have not come to understand this beast.

For even in one's soul, the power that time holds is quite possibly the most powerful influence that can be found. I cannot explain this part without the pressing urge to first clarify that I am completely aware of how absurd it sounds. I feel most of the time as though the struggles that have come along with the short period in which I knew Vergil were not ones that had anything to do with the way I wanted to feel about him. I knew it was wrong. I knew it all along. I did not particularly enjoy the feeling of feeling as though in his absence a part of me was also absent. I felt most of the time as though it was simply a third party controlling me, making me feel these things. I do truly believe that it was, still to this day, my soul doing so. It is the strangest thing. I had the other day, come across a picture of him, and as soon as my eyes made contact with it I felt something inside of me jump very literally. It was a small but very sharp wisp in my chest. It was in that exact moment, that I understood what it all meant. It was my soul. My soul was the one this whole time that had intertwined with him previously in the sands of time.

To be completely frank, I can say that as of yet, I have not ever had this sense or felt this way about another human being ever before in my life. Although it is no lie to say that I do love him, it would be a lie to say that only I did. It is hardest for me now, in trying to describe exactly what I want to say when trying to explain this whole ordeal. I know for certain that I have met him before in a past life. I am however, not certain about the pretences around the prior life. I'd like to imagine it to be something of a beautifully tragic romance, and although it pains me to use the word tragic, it is the word that fits. No matter how many times I go through it all over again in my mind, I am left with the haunting reality that there might be no possible way to now, as it stands a finished ordeal, revitalize the love that might have succeeded if its periodization in time had been correct. Time has taken much from me, but I never thought that it would have succeeded in taking the same thing from me twice. I loved this man, and in not only one, but two life times, I had not been successful in achieving happiness. Did I not learn from my mistake?

There are many different things that I regret either doing or not doing. The one and single thing that I regret the most basically, is having let time win for the second interval. It was apparent to both Vergil and I that when we entered each other's lives, their paths would have led to something completely different than the direction they were headed prior to it. I humour myself in thinking of how extremely unique the whole situation was for both him and I. Often, I forget to try and understand his perspective about the whole set of events, but to be completely honest, I think it is only present where it is relevant. I was simply the girl that he did not love from having loved and lost so many others before me. And he was simply the boy in which I fell in love with. The only person I have ever loved, and might ever love, for eternity. I am not sure that even before meeting him, I would have ever believed that one could love someone with such conviction as I loved him. Now, I understand it as the being only possible way to live my life in happiness.

I wish I could so easily have moved on with my life. Fallen in love again, and have enjoyed the years of youth that I had left in peace. This could never happen, because of what had already happened. My soul wants him more than anything. Personally, I have no issue in hoping that with enough hard work and progress, time might allow the day where Vergil and I are together to come. My issue lies only in the deepest crevice of my soul that knows that since the mistake has already been made, that such an ending might only come around in the next life. Not to say that this is the reason explaining all of my sorrow and sadness. No, such emotions lie in the fact that I shall spend this life using every single aspect that I can to make it as possible for me to be with him as I can. I believe that success comes ultimately, to those who choose wait for it, or those who choose to speed up and meet it in its path if they are not patient. For it is the things that take the longest time, that are the ones worth doing. If it takes me three lives to have completed my task, so be it. I understand this waiting and passing of time only as a figment that will make the end result all the more satisfying.

Certainly, the time was not right for me to have been with Vergil. I was simply still a child when we had met, still so unaware of the disappointment and the hate that filled this world. And he being all too overfilled with emotions that he did not want, with all the sadness and the sorrow that came with having loved and lost. Each to their own. Each by themselves tragic characters. Together they created nothing but the entity of polar opposites with the same ending. For now, I choose to believe that a day will come where happiness will find us. Where the cloud of darkness will have been lifted and the only thing dark will be the shadows that the sun will cast of our body walking in a field of flowers holding hands and being ecstatic that happiness had finally found both of us. When happiness has found us, when success is all but our embodiment, I truly believe that I will have achieved all that I ever wanted, and that my soul, and his, will be set free.

Effects Within the Inconsistencies of Time

As I have previously established, I do not hold the most favourable relationship with time since it has not been kind to me in the past, and I dare say, is currently set on inflicting the same sort of damage in this life also. Within my contract, time has come to have had many more effects than I thought it might have had since my last life, some beneficial, others crippling. Not to say that I did not expect for time to have changed the way everyday life is lived, but rather the way in which these changes in our society have come about, and the effects that have yet to surface in their establishment, are the ones that have taken me by surprise.

There are certain elements, certain things in history that have recently come to change in the present day, and I believe that it is these discrepancies, these changes, that will come to shape the current generation differently then any other previous generation. With change comes the implementation of new ideas. However it is the through the lens of the past that these new ideas are and have always been shaped. If this lens was wrong, or rather it if was a lens that was never considered as being such before, then in its changing there would be significant effects. It is in the present day that I have come to conclude that the lens is currently just being established, and it is through this changing of perceptions, or ideals, whose effects have yet to surface. The ideal of change over time seems so linear, so complete in my mind that it comes as one great difficulty for me to try and explain in words for all to comprehend and conclude upon also.

To try and paint this picture as clear as I can, I'd like to give the example of the changing of the seasons to establish the exact meaning of this concept of change over time. In relevance to my own story, the seasons have definitely played an influential role in establishing the intense feelings that I developed for Vergil; I am certain of this. In this life we met each other in the cool midst of spring. As the flowers bloomed in the warm showers of the morning dew, the seasons marked its changing to summer. Just as it seems all tales of hopeful romance do, the elusive summer season crept into the air and so did my love for Vergil. There was something about that summer air, about the easiness of life in the summer, that made it impossible to hate anything. Unconditionally at this point, I loved Vergil. The summer sowed the seeds of regret and change for it was not until the bitter northern cold set in that I realized the roots of my feelings. As Vergil slowly set on his way, departing from my life, I realized the full impact that the summer had on me. It facilitated this love; it made it all the more easier to accept, to believe.

It was easier to say yes to long summer night car rides and having drinks on the beach during the intense heat of its midst. It never occurred to me that in doing so, in having a fun summer with Vergil that I might fail to realize exactly how hard I had fallen for this man. Just as the summer facilitated the blooming of my love for him, the winter frosted any sort of love he might have evaded in realizing over these summer months. When, old man winter came around, I realized that I had loved him, since in his absence all my mind could do was wander towards him and think about him, about the shadows that lurked now in the summer's past. He realized this too, perhaps not on the same scale as I did, for Vergil was the only man I had ever loved, but he knew only that many memories were made that summer, and that I had tried my absolute best to have made it memorable.

Presently still, a season has yet to melt into another where I didn't find myself thinking about Vergil and that summer we spent together learning what the definitions of folly and joy were. Perhaps the more accurate thing to state would be my learning of what those things were, since I didn't know what any of it meant to him. I take to believing that it most certainly meant less to him than he did to me, which as time has come to prove to me, is wrong and undesirable in this present day. This begins then, to shape another example that can be used to explain exactly what I mean to say about the changing of time at a faster rate than possible for the human race to have realized the effects in its unfolding.

Somewhere along the line, as I am certain it has not occurred within the time that I have been alive, love has come to know a different definition than it had in the past, which is one of the reasons that I quarrel with it so. The conflict that I have agreed to solve in the contract of this life established itself in another first. What love was, what it is depicted as in this life, and how it is now expressed between other human beings is something that I do not understand. It is defined now through meaningless sexual relations with others, in money and disloyalty. The sensitivities of love are traits that have come to evolve as something much different in this time and I have yet to conclude on whether or not these changes in perception can be labelled as a catalyst that will evolve in time as a problem, or rather simply that the concept of love as humans have known it, has matured to the next stage of its life as we comprehend it. Either being the case, I am not happy with it. Either way, it almost eliminates the possibility of my love for Vergil being strong enough to break the contract he holds with the Devil in regards to his soul, and also the possibility of my soul finally being able to reach its next stage of maturity, whatever that may be.

To be quite honest, this love that I have for him and the power I believe it to hold is not entirely a creation solely based on his magnificence. No, it relates also to the fact that it isn't just his soul that is in question here. Mine is too. Even if the role that his soul plays is only to allow for my soul to become complete once more, which isn't the case because I love this man and value him just as much as I do my own half of the soul, I do not think it is right for anyone to say that I should not be able to do so, to have a complete soul. The love that I have for him seems to be useless in this time; a fact that I did not think would even have been present let alone holding more validity than that of holding timeless love with value and regard.

I have read stories and have grown up believing that love was something beautiful, something that made life seem almost as though it should have been described right out of a book. It was something timeless, and it was known that it could conquer all. Apparently, love has evolved past this, for now the belief that affection and emotion towards another are labelled as wrong because they rely on putting the daily strength that allows you to live happily into another person. Why was that wrong?

I cannot help but think of medieval maidens falling into the arms of their ever so perfect princes exemplifying how life seems incapable of living when they are out to war. Or even the famous example of two lovers who killed themselves because the social conventions of the society they lived in did not allow for them to be together exemplifies this sort of ancient power. This period in time allows for no such stories of love to exist. Love has lost its traditional values of reliance and singularity, only to pick up other qualities like intensity and the speed at which it ferments and fades. Its not that it has lost its meaning entirely, but the concept of love has certainly changed since the last time my soul embodied a corpse on this earth, I am certain of it. I personally do not like the new characteristics of love, for they work against me in my quest. Others I am sure, have found relief in these new characteristics for the power of love most certainly is much more equally distributed between the sexes within this time, which as a female, is nice to see.

This being true has also put me in a strange position to be in because for the first time, I have been negatively labelled by society because I do not follow the conventions of not being an extension of the person whom you have fallen in love with. We scream individuality and impersonality. Those who have such qualities are praised and desired by an immeasurable amount of others, who ultimately, seek to acquire the same characteristics in their character. They spend countless amounts of dollars and countless hours to achieve this end, to establish themselves as an individual who does not rely on anyone except for them self. This evolution of society, this warping of conventions in time, has led me to understand just how useless and wrong my love for Vergil is. It isn't the fact that I love him that is wrong, it is how much love him, how much of myself I would unthinkingly give to him, and all that I would sacrifice for his happiness that is wrong. But I wondered why this was.

Why was it wrong to feel that way about anyone? Who was given the right to dismiss the source of another's strength so easily, so carelessly, and so quickly? Clingy, needy, and dramatic are just a few of the negative words that others have come to inflict upon me in trying to tell them just how intensely and surely the feelings I felt about Vergil were. The words mad, insane, and crazy have been added more recently to the mix. Only more recently so because as I have told them of his constant presence in my mind, of his festering there also, I have been pleaded with by many a friend to change these feelings as soon as I possibly could. Some even went as far as to insist that I seek medical aid, for not only was it wrong for me to felt this way about another human being, but it was also unhealthy to do so. I do not, nor will I ever consider anyone telling me these things to be wrong, for I did not believe that they were, even though I viewed the situation much differently myself. Was it possible for both of us to be right? I wondered whether or not someone had to be wrong in this situation.

All of these things they told me about how I felt, were not only as true as the feelings that I had for Vergil, but they were hurtful also. My silent love for Vergil and belief in this whole story never hurt anyone else, not like the words of others directed towards me did. I felt for the first time as though in living my life in this fashion, even if I was only able to live as an extension of his shadow, it still seemed that I lived much more happily than I had ever done so in my life before. What then, was so wrong with that? And as simply as it had been contested, the answer to such a question became all too apparent. It was the time in which we lived in. This was simply the way it was, but was not for me. It was this isolation of feelings on my behalf, the feelings that I had that were relatable to the feelings of no one else on this earth presently in this time, that could be found as the only negative aspect of my feelings towards Vergil. We see the time of the present blend into the future, everyday right in front of our eyes, and no one has yet to question it as it does so. As I stand alone on this subject, and like many others, I find myself asking how the feelings that I have for Vergil that have permitted me to continue living, could ever have been labelled as wrong?

Perhaps it is because that they were once considered as all too right. It was only the role of a woman to have existed through the hand of a man, for the world revolved around the sun only to meet their needs and not the needs of others, of women, or even of the individual. At least, this was the case of how it was in the last life spent between Vergil and I. It was much different now, that was for certain. It was these discrepancies within the effects of time that I have been so quick to label in a negative light for they have surely lessened the rate that I might have success in this daunting task I have been held to complete. Even though these changes can be deemed as negative with respects to the task given to fulfill and complete my soul, there must also be a lens through which they can equally be seen as positive.

The most evident and obvious positive effect of this equality is surely the equality between the sexes in terms of rights, employment, and overall everyday life. That was positive because in the least this life had not filled my mind with images and realities of inequality between men and women. It was certain that in the past this was an aspect of my life that had not been present, so even though I found it still to be a positive aspect of this new social order, I believed it to be something that added difficulty to my everyday life because I knew not exactly how to function through this lens of equality. Every life I have lived, which may or may not have been more than the one I recollect now through Vergil, has unfolded through this lens of male superiority; so you too see now just how new and up turning this life has come to be for me in simply trying to exist and understand all of the differences that have developed since last I lived on this earth. It just personally seemed that this evolution which has taken place since the last time I met Vergil have unfolded at a rate that was too rapid for my soul to have adjusted to it accordingly.

However, it was not just my lack of being able to adjust to the changes that bothered me. It was that I was either alone in feeling that humans have took to evolve these characteristics at a pace that is too fast for my soul to adjust too, making me the only one affected by this, adding only to my misplacement in this time, or that it was not just me and that I have seen and identified an inconsistency of time that others have overlooked. This seemed as far fetched as the warped reality that I lived in now through Vergil and my conquering love for him. No, I think more likely it is not only I that have come to be affected by these changes. Surely there had to be at least one other soul on this earth besides my disgracefully incomplete half that found themselves feeling this way. I couldn't have been alone. I was not willing to accept that as an option. There had to be someone else who thought that the evolution of love and its characteristics were occurring at a rate so fast that the human spirit had not the capability to adapt to it so readily as it occurred.

My mind has surely wandered off topic and into matters that cannot be discussed without the input of any personal opinions on controversial subjects that I'd prefer to rather not have any input on. Putting this quarrel with the evolution of love aside, there are surely a few other aspects to this life that I can find positive in the shadows of its negative brother. One was that it was possible to live as an individual, meaning that you lived only for yourself and not as an extension of another person allowing ultimately, completely autonomy within the city and time one lived in. As much as I hated that this was indeed a positive fact because I no longer had the option of living as an extension of Vergil and as a complete soul, it was still nice to know that even though this was no longer my reality, that such a lack of, could be adjusted and mended within the social conventions of this time.

Lastly, this time has come to show me that there might have been time for me to complete this terribly daunting end task. If time has allowed itself to fast forwards natural evolution of human creations through time, then something as surreal as actually being successful in getting Vergil's his half of soul back from the Devil might actually be possible. I think, most likely, that it was this possibility that made me carry on living in this time day after day. Everything that occurs in our lives has done so for a specific reason, even if we do not come to realize its significance. I was certain that all of the things that were different in this time, that facilitated the opposition's will, might also have been exactly what I needed to reassure myself of just how certain I was that my soul could succeed in this task.

On Human Nature

Not to say that a chapter focusing on an a subject as universally applicable as the nature of our species as humans is not one that shouldn't exist within these pages, but rather I'd like to address the fact that it is a subject that could be argued as not relevant to the story, which would make its place here irrelevant also. Even before I start I'd like to clarify exactly why such a chapter as this one does in fact exist within these pages. Simply because it can is the most accurate explanation that I can offer. As it stands currently in time, philosophy and theological concepts of life have only ever come to surface through the lens of a male perspective. To say that all of the varying viewpoints on these subjects are invalid because they are not female or in the least considering of them even is not a valid assumption one can make for it is crass.

Even as it stands currently in time, I do not believe that the view I have to offer on the subject of human nature is one that can be labelled as universal, but it is one that can come to be added into the mix. Since by nature, it is a view point that is labelled as a unique addition to its conceptions because I am a female, the idea of what human nature might actually be comes one step closer to being answered. A completely female point of view adds only to side of what a woman might consider to be the nature of humans, so in itself, my view is incomplete. Nonetheless, it might be possible to forge one complete view that is universally applicable to both genders in time. Sadly, this is not such a view point, for it is only an addition to something that might be considered as such when the time in which the history of males and females stand as equals; although they are en route to such, there is still much time that needs to have elapsed to come to any conclusions of the equality of both men and women.

I am convinced that the answer to the question of what we might be able to label with the title of human nature has already been presented to the human race, yet it simply has been overlooked for its placement all along the entire timeline of our existence. In my ponderings of the question I have ironically come to formulate my answer on it based upon the very ideas I initially questioned. What if human nature is simply that on a timeline, men were always destined to have believed that they were the superior sex in the first place? Then, when the ancient conceptions of their superiority not only to their female counterparts but others who they deemed as subservient, would have been a completely valid conception, it would also come to be the only one that could be proven otherwise as time went on. It their period, in their existence on a timeline, they were not wrong. On our current placement on the same timeline, we have come to put stark into ideas of human nature that seemed to be more revolutionized and current with the time in which we live.

As plainly as I can put it, I believe that human nature is that men were to believe that they were by some force, more deserving of essential life aspects such as politics, history, education, and a general sense of entitlement. That is human nature. If this is true, it does not come to mean much other than the fact that it is what it is until it is placed on the current positioning of the human race on its timeline. Currently, this conception has come to become turned on its head, for both men and women stand as beings of equal worth. Such a phenomenon of equality has only come about in the past few hundred years or so. As we have now become equals to that of our fellow man, the place that a woman holds in the present society is one that has never been had before. Now that we have been deemed worthy of being associated with equal importance to our fellow man, this is surely a marker in history. A fact that as a woman, I feel very blessed to have since it was something that many before me had not. We shall never come to know of how these women conceived the world, so it is imperative for me now to do so since I have been blessed in my placement on the timeline to have the ability to do so.

Since my conception of human nature is presented using the traditional format of being uniquely applicable to males, I see no reason why this should diminish its level of validity for it follows in the footsteps of history, and to diminish its validity based on this specific one sided aspect would only weaken the ideas of other great thinkers before me. There are two other realities that would then be present. The first of course being that women should have been equal from the start, then such a problem would never have arisen.

I say problem only now because it is an issue that I believe to be one of great importance for I can see presently that it might be within a series of events that will come to have shaped history as we will come to define it tomorrow, or in the future.

The second being the one that we are currently living in also. Now that women have equality to men it obviously states that an entire gender is admitting that they were wrong at least one point in time. I think it is quite amusing to think that no women can be found who can have said about them that they as an entire gender have made the mistake of suppressing its opposition. We as a collective group have the ability to validly say that we do not belong to a selection of humans that can be labelled as having rights over others since the beginning of noted history. I am using the base point of noted history as a unit of measurement to have the ability to conclude that such can also be known as the beginning of time. This of course comes into relation with the element of time and how it functions, and whether or not it is a human creation.

As it exists on a linear scale, not enough time has passed where it is valid to say that both men and women have had equivalent sections of time where they were considered as equals or both as human beings. I mean to say that even though there will always be a larger fragment of time in history where men were seen as the only gender that had the capabilities of reason. However, the human race has come to conceptualize both men and women as equal human beings within the current time period, and I believe that once women come to have equal rights for the same amount of time that only men had rights, it will be during that point in time where the human race might obtain the ability to conclude about what human nature truly is. I am not claiming to have some sort of whimsical insight on this subject, for I am certain that I do not. To develop the idea of something that can be universally applied as the nature of a species is one that I have not attempted here. It has been attempted, and some might even dare to argue succeeded, by many different men before me. Only when each of those who have been deemed deserving of human rights believes that no aspects of life remain where the opposite is true, then the idea of human nature may come to be resolved.

Having said this, I'd like to add that it might be possible that in time, the roles of superiority might actually come to reverse themselves. Wouldn't it be interesting if as time progressed on a linear scale, women would come to be deemed as the gender that is most deserving of daily entitlements? Of course, I am neither hoping nor wanting of such a future, for I believe a large sense of resentment would go along with the future if it did unfold as such. Additionally, it would only come to slow down the advancement of the human species, just as the oppression of women did for some thousand years. If ever a gender wanted to prove that they were superior to another, they might subtly be able to do so in choosing not to retain any ideas of hate or resentment towards the oppressors of their past since they stand now as equals.

Lastly, what if the level of equality now shared amongst the sexes is one that goes against the theory of human nature as I have described it above. It is possible that this would then mean that my theory on human nature is wrong, or it might mean something of a much greater significance. If human nature is that men must live in a setting where they feel superior to those living around them, even if it is purely on a subconscious level, would the present then not interfere with this? I wonder about the implications of living in a society where men and women are considered equals, when in the past it was so clear for such a lengthy period that they were not. Even though the idea of equality is one that I believe to be the main focus on what human nature might actually mean, it is not the sole one that is present.

As a female, I believe that a part of our human nature that has largely gone under looked is that of love. I do not believe that I have ever had the pleasure of reading any ancient texts that mention love as something that is unique to the human species. Although others species find mates and feel connections with them, I believe that there is also a tangible lack of conceptions that forbids them from recognizing the connection they have as anything that cannot be explained as simply being present. Love is a different sort of concept because it is one that we know exists, for it is one that we have also come to label and in a way, it has been allowed to define us. Due to the lack of its information, I deem it the nature of women to be the true informers of its knowledge. If it was to be considered as the affairs of men, surely it would have been done as such already.

Man is a physical animal, not to say that he is not a rational one, but rather to say he has also the power to enforce is will over those of others. Such may be the human nature of a man. A woman might not come as having the same nature. We are both however humans and so therefore there must be something that we both have in common that we can conclude is human nature. Just as men are the ones who would come to define what power and superiority is, women will come to define what love is. As the latter begins to take its place in the current time, I can only come to hope that it is done so in a way that will facilitate the creation of one idea on human nature that is equally applicable to both men and women.

Uncertainty

One step after the other my feet seemed to gain weight making each step harder to take then the last, until finally I came to a standstill. I came to a complete stop, and for the life of me I could think of no reason to take another step. Standing there simply mesmerized, the edge seemed to draw me in. The curiosity of what lay on the other side tempted me. Throwing my suicidal thoughts out of the window that was my mind, I told myself to shut up. A sense of macabre curiosity festered like a virus in within me. There was nothing really stopping me from jumping off this bridge.

However, it was not these thoughts that terrified me so. The hard fact of the matter was that my mind chose to, as a natural reaction, find darkness and thoughts of self-harm. As much as I would like to say that these thoughts had occurred only as I was on this bridge, that would be false, and a liar is one thing that I am not. Currently, the darkness finds me more often than not; I was at one point in my life, almost consistently trying to think of reasons not to kill myself.

This bridge. This moment. Allowing only for me to become aware that the world was a lonely place. I wondered how many people had walked past this bridge, thinking of reasons not to jump? How many of them were female? How many of them presented a content façade on a daily basis to convince everyone around them that the bridge was just a bridge as they walked by it? I tried to imagine, carve, or morph together a person, similar to myself, that would have these thoughts as their reality in walking past this bridge like I was now doing. Unfortunately, my own image was the only creation that surfaced each time. There, I sunk deeper into the deep end, drowning almost in my own figurative tears. Every suicidal thought that could not be silenced with my inner-self giving me a reason to live, started slowly to hack away at my mind. I could not think of one reason. I continued walking. Exhale.

The second time I crossed the bridge my initial reaction was not to slow down and let every macabre thought in my mind ferment. This time as I was passing, I noticed the benches that were positioned a bit too eerily close to the edge of the bridge. Perhaps the distance was two feet, if that. The bridge itself went over the edge of an old track that used to be occupied with the hustle and bustle of a train, a fraction of this city that I have still yet to truly discover. In other words, the bridge was built over a train track, and a walkway that was built to parallel the track. My fascination this time lay not with the tracks of the walkway but rather with the lame benches overlooking the only section of the bridge that could be jumped off of. It might have been just me, but it seemed strange that the benches resided only on this part of the bridge. Why would anyone sit on these benches, when the only view that could be seen was a train and its tracks? There was no way that a logical answer could be found for this anomaly. I looked around as I was passing to see if there was a bus stop, since surely that would have given purpose to these benches. Alas, there was not. Either way, with the benches facing away from the road, it would have raised another question as to why they were like that if they were meant for transit riders.

In passing the bridge, I rested my thoughts on these benches and I tried to place the image of a frail, lonely old woman sitting comfortably enjoying her day holding a bag of seeds, awaiting any hungry bird bellies that would give her the company she had set out to find in sitting on these benches. Seemingly enough, this was a very possibly reality. I could find no reason why a woman fitting that description would not enjoy such activities, especially in the type of neighbourhood this was. It was not a bad neighbourhood at all, really it was genuinely average. I imagined myself sitting on the bench, and I thought about what I could think about. Circumstantially, to the old woman whose aims would be surely to enjoy herself, but another story unfolded before my eyes. I would sit there gazing hopelessly at the tracks, wondering, and hoping that if I jumped, my life would end. The benches seemed to me only a marker of sorrow as they would serve only to my purpose as a way to help me imagine this death over and over again so vividly in my mind. Each time coming closer to the final step, until I would not be able to tell the difference between what was my imagination and what was reality. Inevitably, it would lead to a merging of the two from my lack of being able to distinguish one from another. A shiver went down my spine, and a sense of terror sparked through my soul. For my safety, I didn't think that it would be a swell idea to venture back upon this bridge; a part of me still believed that I had something to live for.

Often, one realizes the instrument of their damnation happens to usually be the instrument of their salvation as well. If it wasn't enough of a cliché already, this happened to be applicable to my situation also. This bridge, which I had only seen in a negative light before, dawned on me as the perfect opportunity the third time I came to pass it. I deemed it as the perfect space to finally find myself. It was my overwhelming feelings of loneliness and isolation that brought me back to the benches on the bridge this time. It was very clear to me that my previous thoughts on the bridge both the first and second time, were uniquely mine. As I am sure that no one before me had thought the same things I did in passing it. It was after all, a bridge. I mean in all seriousness, I cannot think of the quality of character that would think the same thoughts as my mind did in passing it.

I guess the saying "third times the charm" really does apply because as I made the twenty or so minute walk down the street to the bridge, I felt elated. Even before I began the journey to the bridge that night, I was elated to think that my mind had finally reached a condition where it might be so inclined to find a shred of positive light towards it.

It may have been the time of day, or even just a spur in the moment that lead me to feel as committed as I had been to feeling different about this bridge than any of the other times I had crossed it. The negative feelings that I did have, really had no stems that I could identify. I believe that this might have been the origins for my strong convictions to find something different this time. After a reflective walk to it, I reached the bridge, with the current reconciling feelings I had developed for it still intact. I sat down on the benches in silence and refused to allow the darkness to find me. Not to say that it was not there, but rather I made sure that this time, in the least, I had the ability to keep it at bay. That night as I sat there lifelessly staring at the abandoned track below me, I remained rather calm for the sensation of jumping over the edge did not come to me then. Rather, my attention focused on the others crossing the bridge that night. A few of the other souls that had come to pass the bridge that day, not all, took notice of me sitting on the bench. I did not mind that they had, but I did wonder about what sort of thoughts they might have had about the person I appeared to be to them that night. I didn't really care what they thought of me, but I kept my guard up to see if I could notice anyone giving off the same sort of disposition I had the first two times I found myself on this bridge.

Sadly, I did not come to find anyone else who might have felt the same that that I had. My uniqueness and its reactions to the events that occurred in my life had never really come as a surprise. I guess in a way then, it was reassuring that I found no one that was similar to me on the bridge. It would have pained my gravely to try and imagine another being feel the same level of sorrow that I had initially as a by-product of the possibilities that went along with being a presence on the bridge. It was only in the present moment that I understood there were other feelings that were to be had on this bridge also; it didn't have to all be thoughts of suicide, it was only one of the views that could be had.

There were a few others that crossed the bridge that night, and as I looked at them, I noticed they had looks only of unappealing disgust to present me with, and I couldn't give them less regard if I wanted to. This is for the person that dared to find something different and unique in something so average to a normal person or even something so terrifyingly real. Everyone is on a different journey, but we all want the same blissful ending. I put my shoes on. They had cooled down in the cold summer breeze. I thought I was done smiling for the day, but I was elated to have been mistaken.

Illness

I can't remember a point in my life where I have felt as though my health was equivalent to the majority of those around me. Even as a small child, my health seemed to be unfairly poor. Even my older sibling had poor health, although it wasn't quite as bad as mine. When I was just four years old, I developed the most crippling of my diseases, and it has now come to define most of the actions that I execute in my daily life. Everything I do must be monitored, every food item that I consume, every long walk I take in solitude, each coffee I have in the morning; it must all be accounted for.

I've never contemplated my health until now. I've always accepted it as the misfortune that it has always been a part of my life. Not allowing me to eat the same things that other kids ate, having to take my medication at all times of the day, and never truly being able to let my guard completely down since the disease surely never did either. I used to be levels of envious that could very well have been high enough to turn my entire body green, not just my face, of the people around me who had perfect health. I had even more built up anger towards people who had perfect health and because of it, disrespected their bodies because they knew that no harm would come to them for doing so. People that would abuse substances, eat nothing but unhealthy foods, and still have a perfect bill of health. It made me upset. It was ever more upsetting when I tried to contemplate why it seemed that I had been the lucky winner of this poor health lottery as opposed to anybody else. It was only me that needed to take handfuls of medication to survive. To be that person, no matter how bright eyed and bushy tailed you start off in life as, makes you hate living a little bit more each day. I've heard people say before that illness or disabilities are insignificant compared to a bad attitude, however, in all seriousness, I wonder all the time why I am the person that was given all this sickness as opposed to anyone else.

Being ill affects both your physical and mental wellbeing. Mentally, being a sickly child means that no matter where you are living, it will always take a significantly longer amount of time for you just to simply exist compared to everyone else on the Earth. Normally, these shouldn't be a problem since it is what it is and there is nothing that can be done about it. If it takes me five minutes extra each morning because I have to take my medications and make sure everything in my body is functioning as it should, well then there really isn't much that I can do about it and I shouldn't be getting upset over something that I cannot control. But there is also another side to this. If you have been brought up in a culture that does not value you significantly enough that you feel important enough to deserve taking care of yourself, then you start to neglect your body simply because you can. Often I have felt that there is such a large and drastic amount of things that I must do simply to exist, let alone prosper, that I do not deserve to be alive. Most of the time, I feel as though my life is a unique experience, unlike any other person, and that I have been struck with this terribly functioning body which I am sure is part of the reason why intense feelings of isolation have formed in my mind. I hate the fact that I am alive only because I have taken handfuls of medication, which in turn, has only caused me to hate myself even more.

A few times I have gotten so fed up to the point where I have refused to take any medication for some extended periods of time. Not only does this physically affect my health, but mentally I feel terrible also. Even more so terrible mentally when I realize just how dependent my body is on these medications. As the tears flowed down my cheeks I thought of how much pain and suffering being ill has caused me throughout the years.

Yet it is nothing compared to the levels of pain I experienced in having to let you go. I have always blown out my birthday candles and wished that I would one day have the opportunity to not be a sick person anymore. However, the last time I made a birthday wish it was to have the opportunity to be given another chance at being an acceptable match for you in your eyes. I laugh because I know now that both are equally unrealistic. I will never be given another chance to be with you, and I will exist solely as an extension of my medications. A fate I find perhaps even more terrible than death.

To know that no matter what, even if you take care of yourself the best that you can, you will not ever live past the age of fifty. That is the harsh reality that I live with every day. If I do not take care of myself, then the number will be even shorter. As someone who is currently quite young, yet seemingly elderly at the same time, with a life that is almost half done, it often causes me to lose hope in my existence. What is the point in living if you know that truly your life will not have been lived to the fullest, that you will have died before your time, and that there is absolutely nothing that you can do to change that? I lose hope thinking about my health. Coincidentally it is the hope of one day being able to say that I am happy in your arms that keeps me getting through the days. In reality I know that like my hopes of living a life that is longer than was meant for me is as futile as the first idea of being yours; but at least it is something. I need something to go on, something to believe in, since believing in myself has always been completely out of question.

Mental effects of illness are only one aspect of its festering. It affects the physical also as harshly since obviously, being ill means that there is a part of your body that isn't working as it should be. Physical implications of being a sickly person are usually ones that can be seen with the naked eye, like pale skin or dark circles under your eyes. Do not get me wrong, I am ever so happy that my soul has been given the opportunity to live this life as fully as it can, for only a mere seventy years prior, I would not have lived past the age of five. Currently, all of my illnesses have a way where it is possible for me to live, albeit with a tremendous amount of effort and work. I have come to the conclusion that curiously enough, my illnesses have somewhat of a plausible explanation. One that, in the least, makes sense enough to me to not mind what any other explanation that might be presented could have to say.

I believe that all of my illnesses are simply the conditions in which my soul had to agree to in order to be given the chance at this life. For whatever reason, the life that my soul lived last had been very difficult, and its ending was not anymore pleasant. I am covered with birthmarks, some as large as the size of a tennis ball. In a past life, something had occurred to me in death that caused these markings to become permanent scars on my present body. To think that everyone has their own destiny and predetermined route that they think is not something that I can discredit entirely because it is the only theory that I have been able to expand upon as an explanation for my conditions that does not make me feel terrible to be alive. With this explanation at least I feel as though my life, no matter how unfortunate my health may get, it is simply something that is beyond my control and because of it, I should not feel bad for being as sick as I am. I deserve to live, or at least, I do for now.

My poor health is the result of my soul not having had the proper amount of time to heal since the last time it inhabited a body. I was given an ultimatum as a soul. The conditions for trying to finally accomplish what I was meant to do came up and I was given two different options to choose from; I could take the punitive conditions that came along with being a soul that was not fully healed, or I could wait again until the next opportunity became available for my soul to finally complete the task that it was destined to do in order to finish. I know the type of soul that I am, for I chose the initial option. I did not want to wait to fully heal, for the next set of conditions to occur that would allow my soul to achieve its goal. Interestingly enough, I did not come to think about the repercussions of judgment that might come along from the general public with respects to inhabiting an ill body. I did not think either about the repulsion that would accompany the feelings of any individual that I might come to know personally. I believe that even still, it might be possible to move on after this life has come to pass. In saying this I mean that every soul has a purpose, a specific ending that they must eventually get to in order to move onto its next stage. However, even though each life that a soul passes through is meant to give the same opportunities as the previous one, it is only through destiny that a soul might finally come to achieve their final and only goal.

As a hopeful romantic, I am inclined to believe with all my heart that this ultimate end goal would be to find one's true love. Not just a love of one's life, but the love of their lives. The soul that this person could embody would then, no matter any sort of present material explanation, have your heart forever. It is the person that you think of when you are falling asleep, the person that you think about when you awaken, and the person that will always be the perfect person for you. Often, I feel as though such an intense connection with another would lead one to take further action in perusing the other, but I have recently learned otherwise. It is not that the other person didn't feel the same connection; it is that the timing was simply not right. It is nothing short of the most terrible of tragedy when this occurs. The two might be perfect for each other, and yet, something has rippled the sands of time and caused life to unfold in such a miserable way.

This is what happened with you Vergil. I have only ever understood it as this type of situation. I wanted nothing more in the world than for you to feel like you were just as perfect as I saw you. I hoped with all my heart that time had not made its mark on you, but I know that it had already even before I met you. I hate myself for not having been good enough to make you feel differently about me than any of the other females who have made you feel as though you are not good enough. I hate knowing that if I had met you maybe even a year or two later, that our encounters would have been different, that I might have had a chance. Unfortunately it is not only a reflection of you, but also one of me. I have always been the girl to get ahead of herself. To be eager and wanting of everything, without processing the ability to be patient and wait for it. I wanted to have a chance with you when I did, when I was young, and when you were broken. I took my leave from your life in the hopes of forgetting all that you have done to me, all that you made me feel. Of course, my efforts continue to be futile. Just as my soul chose this life over waiting for the next, I am eager to do it right this time. I feel as though our paths will cross again, and I know that if they ever do, it will be different. This time, I will be perfect for you also.

There is a scenario in my mind that seems to be replay over and over again no matter how many times I try not to think about it, or you. We live in the same city my love, just as I am certain that it was your soul that brought me to this city, I am sure that our paths will cross once more. We shall be walking down the street and I will look onto you, and you onto me. I know not what my reaction will be, for I know that all I would ever want to do would be to fall into your arms. I do not know if when such a day comes, I will have the ability to simply walk past you indifferently. I want to want to do so, but I simply cannot. I will never come to understand the reasons why it was made impossible for me to be with you in this lifetime. My love, it is true when I say that I simply could never come to being myself and to give up on you. Just as my illness has come to define me since childhood, you have come to define my very existence as a soul living within the body of a female.

The Woman at the Hospital

Surely from past experiences, my feelings towards hospitals and their situations in time as settings have always been quite disagreeable. I have never been one to express excitement in receiving the knowledge that I was due to the hospital, no matter what reason. When I was a small child, I had many different experiences that took place at the hospital, usually elapsing over a period in time that was more than just a quick visit with the doctor. I always left the hospital feeling fine, but usually only as a by-product of being put on another medication, or some other less pleasant alternative. Many do not like the idea of hospitals, mainly because of the anxiety that is commonly associated with them, due to whatever personal reason that makes sense to them. For me, this was no exception, and my reasons were plentiful. However, one night when I was at a hospital for the birth of an acquaintance's first child, a very strange event took place. I tried for a moment to change what the suppositions about hospitals were to a woman whom I knew nothing about who had approached me whilst I was awaiting the bus. To this woman I could have chosen to say anything, and in reality, it shocked me ever so deeply that I choose to take the route that expressed how the hospital was not the gravest of places, even though I would have been more truthful in expressing the exact opposite to her.

The bus stop was quite a ways from the hospital, about a ten minute walk. It could very well have been that the closest bus stop was not the one I had chosen to wait at that night, but I did not know of any other stop, and in the dead of evening, I was not prepared to get lost. Walking and simply enjoying the mildness of the inviting summer weather has always been something that I've appreciated doing, and this evening was no exception to this. I listened to some lovely scenic music in traveling to my destination, and when I reached it, I was absolutely calm and simply in an intoxicatingly content mood.

From the corner of my eye a woman caught my attention. She was walking towards me at quite an aggressively fast pace. It could have been described rather accurately as almost running. It was certain that she was in a rush. I turned my head to look behind me. My mind came to the logical conclusion that the bus had been on its way, and in seeing this, she wanted to ensure that she would make it to the bus on time. This was not the case, for the street remained illuminated only by the dim streetlights that made their homes on the sidewalk. I turned back to the woman who was a much more considerable amount closer to me, and it became clear now that she was strictly looking at me. My concern grew only in realizing that she was clenching a stuffed bear close to her heart, and appeared to be crying. She was wearing a night down, which simply by the location of where we both were, could have been found as oddly out of place since most people only wear their nightgowns to bed. It was night time though, so I didn't think much too much about her garbs.

Initially, a small sense of terror and fear overcame me; then a small but concentrated jolt was sent up my spine. I believe that this was the result of having been so calm and serene before the woman's upheaving arrival. It was not the usual scene one would expect to see in waiting for the bus, especially when the day has given way to the darkness of the evening. As the woman's eyes met mine, I knew at that moment that there was no possible way for me to evade any confrontation with her. She was much larger than me both vertically and horizontally, and although I could easily have protected myself in the case of any physical contact, I was rested assured by the look of uncomfort that rested on her face. It was not any sort of threatening look, it was very mild in fact, but it was also very sad.

She was now next to me and I could see that if anything, this was a woman whom at one point in her life had known happiness and was now on the other side of having had it taken away from her. Entirely distressed, her tears marked their stains on the wrinkles of her cheeks as well as the collar of the night gown she was wearing. She held onto the bear as though it meant something to her, with a very intense passion. She started to speak about how she was mentally ill and that she came here, to the hospital, to check in, but that they had refused to give her any treatment.

To myself I thought this was very strange because I personally, have never been refused medical treatment when I was in need of it at any of the hospitals I have ever ventured to. The woman and I then started our conversation from this starting point. My goal by the end of the conversation was to simply calm her down and perhaps if it was possible, to help her evade any judgment that might be placed upon her by the fellow citizens that would be on the bus when it came. In all honesty, it was difficult to understand quite a bit of what she was saying. Her words were disconnected and muffled by her tears and sniffling nose. She was certainly upset at the hospital and I made it very clear to her that if what she was telling me about them refusing her was in fact the truth, then I believed that she had been wronged. She broke further down into tears, and clasped her teddy bear even tighter. She told me about how she had been abused her whole life and now while she was here waiting for the bus, that she was scared of having to take it all the way home by herself.

Earnestly, I had been completely content with listening to my music before the woman decided that I was to be her target of emotional expellation for the evening. However, I somewhat understood the feelings that she was going through and I did want to help her out the best that I could, whilst at the same time of course, not causing any physical, mental, or emotional distress unto myself. I talked to her for quite a few minutes, simply speaking to her about the different things that always made me feel better when I was feeling sad. I plainly expressed to her that I really did not know how she was feeling because I had never experienced the problems that she told me about. She understood just how unequipped I was to deal with the emotional issues that she was having, but nonetheless, thanked me for trying to help her out the best that I could.

She wanted me to stay with her because she was scared of being alone. I found this exceptionally strange because if ever I could say that I had a preference for something it was to be alone. I did not understand what her reasoning was for being scared of being alone. It seemed that there were only two logical reasonings, the first being that she was scared of the way others might treat her, or she was scared of the direction her thoughts would take if she was left alone without anyone to distract them. If the latter was the case I do believe that talking to me was one of the best decisions that the woman could have ever made. I let her know that by the end of this encounter she would be fine, that if she could have rested assured of anything within this night of uncertainty, it was that she had picked the best possible person to converse with. She smiled at me for the first time. She did not have much exuberance to her smile, but she did have a smile that certainly displayed much more distress than my smile could ever have offered. I told her that by the end of this conversation I hoped that she would have been able to understand that she would most likely never see me again and that it was not to be taken poorly because she would know that this meeting was everything that it needed to be. She was at a rough patch in her life and someone was there to try and understand exactly what she was dealing with. Of course, none of what I had been telling her was really all that true. Even myself, I find it hard at times to hold in all of the tears that I keep locked deep in the crevices of my soul.

I envied the woman a bit on the basis of this principle. She had so openly and vulnerably poured her heart out to me, her tears, and her soul. I wished for a moment that I had the strength to cry in front of a complete stranger. She made sadness look so easy, so uncaring, so unbothered by the world that was around her.

After I was done my attempt of consoling her, she looked at me and slowly let go of the tight clench she had around the teddy bear. She slowly raised the arm that she was now holding the teddy bear with and offered it to me. Such an action as this truly shocked me. I could not believe that she was offering me the only thing that I could see, she tangibly owned. It was not more than two seconds ago that she was gripping onto this bear as if it was made of solid gold. I looked at her with the most compassionate of looks, for I understood what it meant for her to offer me such an article. I simply put my hand out in front of her and told her that she needed to keep the bear for herself. I was only a shadow that she ran into one night waiting for a bus; she didn't have to offer me anything. By the time our conversation was over, she would understand exactly why I did not want to accept her offering. I was planning on sitting next to her on the bus when it came. If anything, this woman needed a friend, even if it was only for a moment of her life.

Personally, I had only a few bus stops to go on the route, which wasn't nearly as far as she had to go. I was completely fine with spending those few stops chatting with her about aimless things like the weather. By the time the bus came she was in much better sprits. She was smiling and was no longer crying. At least ten minutes had passed in waiting for the bus, and when it finally did peek its front around the corner, I could no longer tell at a glance that the woman had been crying at all. She had wiped away the tears and it seemed that she was ready to move on with the present, leaving the past behind. As the bus turned the corner I asked her if she would be okay on the bus; if she thought she could handle being around the people that were on the bus. She told me that she believed she would be fine, and I told her that everything would in fact be, and that it was imperative she not become upset because most of the time getting upset would only make the situation worse. She agreed with me again, and the bus pulled up to the stop.

I got on the bus first and slowly walked to the back and picked out a pair of seats for us to sit in. As I turned around and sat town to greet the woman to the seat I picked out for her next to me, I realized that she was not behind me. I had thought that she was simply going to follow me to the seats. I looked around me on the bus and tried to find her to sit down next to her, however she was nowhere to be found. She did not get on the bus. As the bus drove away, I expected to see her at the bus stop waiting for the other bus route, for it was possible that the bus she needed to take to get home was not the one that I had gotten on. However in this moment, there was not a single soul waiting in the bus shelter as my eyes passed it.

First Impressions

If there is one phrase that I tend to make note of in my life, it is that you truly only ever get one chance to make a first impression. This is absolutely true. However, in this age, this idea or notion can be further expanded upon, for humans have now developed the ability to look at such a situation a bit differently and I'd like to propose that now there may be more than one chance to make a first impression. As a random example, let us examine the case of someone with multiple personality's disorder. Based on the personality of the person's different presented characters, the possibility exists to have been meeting a different person each time and perhaps you would hold a different impression of cet person based on the meetings of each different personality. Interestingly enough, such an example serves only to prove the impressionability of the person whom the impression is being had by. Meaning to say, no matter how many different people that person meets, no matter how many personalities others meet, the point remains that there will never be a situation where the person with multiples personalities would look different. They may act different, causing the person meeting them to hint at a new first impression, but only to the person with the disease does the first impression come as entirely new. Even so, this period in time has permitted the opposite to become a plausible notion also. One has the opportunity, in theory that is, to alter the way they look to the point where another first impression can be had by one single person.

Let me then present a more logical answer to this question. People more and more in this period in time are altering the way that they look. Tattoos and piercings are most prominent example that I am compelled to use. It is this time in history where I would say that a large majority of the population has a tattoo, a piercing, or both. Everyone has them. They are now more common than they have ever been. I think it would surely be safe to say that today bears the possibility of altering yourself to look as differently as you want. Not solely via the two exemplified methods either. One may dye their hair a different colour, or even get surgery to alter their looks to the point where they might become unrecognizable even to people who might have known them their whole life.

One could then, in essence, change the way they looked quite significantly and you might then be able to make more than one first impression if the person that you were meeting did not initially recognize you. They would have thought that you were someone different and in meeting them, the person would have seen a different person, so you would then have made another first impression. As an example, if you had met someone in the earlier years of your life, and they looked young, sweet, and full of life, but then again at a later time they had changed their physical appearance, you might be inclined to meet them once more. If that same person, during the period in which you were not in contact decided to get many different body tattoos, change their hair colour, or even get plastic surgery to alter the way that they looked then in the very least significant and simple of ways, superficially, one would certainly have the chance to make another first impression.

Another aspect that I believe could be taken into account for being able to successfully execute another first impression is weight. Everyone in their life I am sure can think of one person they have known that they did not recognize after a significant weight loss. Weight fluctuations, for some reason are a very good at making people look different whether it is as the result of being caused by any loss of it or gain of it. A significant weight gain, I imagine, would result in the ability for one to open up the possibility of making another first impression on the person which they were impressing upon if they were unable to recognize them, even if only initially.

I guess it must be clarified then as to what is in a first impression, or rather, what is at risk in making a poor first impression. Generally speaking the people in which one has met firstly by making a really horrid first impression might not be considered a relationship as apt for survival as opposed to ones that were started with a notable or positive first impression. It's possible that meeting someone for the first time and making a poor first impression would lead to the ultimate end of the relationship in question if no excitement or notoriety had been taken down by either receiving party when the encounter took place. At least this is what I would like to believe was a catalyst that led to the eventual demise of your presence in my life. It is on the basis of imagining reasons for these terrible feelings or sorrow and loss that are overwhelming my body, which have now begun filling even the darkest and most controlled aspects of my earthly presence. It does not seem entirely invalid for my mind, due to whatever reason, to assume that it was my poor first impression that had something to do with both the beginning and end of this ordeal.

I long for the day where I might get another chance to be in the grace of your presence, to impress you for once. I assume ultimately that I got ahead of myself, as I seem to always do, and this life shall not grant me another opportunity to present myself to you once more. For now, I will never forget the moment where our eyes locked for the first time, intertwining our fates; all pasts, presents, and futures of it. The very moment that you had materialized in front of my acknowledging eyes, a part of me jolted. I can describe it as a small zip inside of my chest that pulled me instinctively toward you, as if it was not my choice to have been so awed by the person who beheld all of this attraction.

I know for certain I did not have the same effect on you. I can say this with a freighting amount of validity, for I know I was in no position to be making any sort of inexplicably magical first impressions that day. Any day spent wearing a uniform working for minimum wage was at that time at least for me, no reason to get excited or prepared. No makeup on my face and of course I was at that time slightly overweight compared to the average weight of this city's inhabitants from what I observed. I wish I had looked presentable that day, even if I would only have had the basic foundations of self-confidence and a respectable visage, things might have ended differently. You might have been more interested in me from the start.

As sad as it is, a rule that has always surrounded the inhabitants of this world is that beauty benefits those who have it, and even those who are able to imitate it. Beauty, although found both in the eyes of the beholder and the beheld equally, remains largely a product that when tangibly noticed by the beholder, can alter the way in which one addresses another. Beauty has the ability to stop the mind in its tracks, and to derail its thoughts. I know this only simply from personal experience, as mine does just this in gazing upon your perfection, whether it be for the first time, the last time, or every time. Unlike anything or anyone I had ever laid my eyes upon before, you stand as the very definition of perfection.

The subconscious qualities that lure our minds to what they perceive as beauty are inexplicably what usually attract us to others throughout our lives. Meeting you was different for it was not beauty, and I did not behold it. Something occurred, but it was not your impeccable beauty that did it. It was not the way that your eyes caught the dim lighting, reflecting a sea of uncertainty into my soul, it was not the way that your hair became ever so emboldened in a fantastically coarse and tamed shinning fashion, it was something else. Whether I can say that it was my feelings of being drawn to you that caused this connection or your absurdly fantastical everything, I cannot say. Really, I do not think it matters, because in my deepest of promises I can say safely that there was a connection that I felt to you, and I know that was true.

I had wished I could also say with such a convicted certainty that I had the same effect on you. I know that I didn't. In due course, I would like to believe that perhaps this was all supposed to happen. I believe this because it is the only series of things that has ever occurred to me that has caused me to understand just how concretely I can say that I feel as though there is no other possible logical way that this could have unfolded to be found. Sometimes I sit in sheer solitude starting at the wall pondering how it might have occurred differently if I had simply been a little bit prettier or a little bit skinnier or more desirable through some other superficial aspect that would have held your affections.

Most of these thoughts only surface as anxieties, but I do not hold them with any less validity because they exist only in my mind. I ponder then about how, with a little luck, I might one day get the opportunity to give you another first impression. An idea like that seemed almost instantly to burrow into my soul. The idea of being able to meet you again for the first time without feeling as though any of my presentation was compromised sends shivers not just up my spine, but throughout my entire body. A feeling so scary and interesting because I know that I live in a world where the possibility to make another first impression exists. It is very difficult for me to grasp the fact that this might be the life that I am given the opportunity to be with you. Of course, as the fulfillment of any soul would, it stands as very difficult and I would have to work very hard for it. Then, if I truly in my heart of hearts wanted to, if I lived my life in the fashion of its success every day, then I might get to do it all over again with you; a fresh and new starting to this whole affair would be possible.

I experience an influx of so many emotions every time I think about the effects you had on me from the start. Even before I met you, I always truly did believe that first impressions were a significant part of the relationships we build throughout our lives. Now, I somewhat understand exactly why that had always been something I thought of, yet never truly had an explanation as to why I thought it. It had never been a thought that could have been associated with a physical explanation before I met you. In knowing you, I can now comprehend such an explanation to the presence of similar if not identical, circumstance in a life before. Simply to clarify, I wish to emphasize that I do not mean to say that the life I am currently living is the same as one that I lived in the past. No, time has ensured that no such thing could ever have the possibility of existing. But what I am saying is that this life, these set of circumstances, the feelings I have and the events and their outcomes that have come to define me, have occurred before. The ending is the same, and from what I gauge has been the same for quite some time now. However, the story leading up to it is different.

Is it possible for something as simple as a first impression to have such a significant and important meaning in any sort of tangibly measurable way that can explain why I feel like this since it is the only first impression that has seriously made me question my existence to the point where I have almost gone completely mad? I want to find some sort of explanation that could help me understand the madness that I experienced in thinking about the first time I acknowledged your existence and you, mine. I need to believe this means something; that there is something worth remembering here. For now, I can conclude only from having known you, that a first impression is something that can bear an immeasurable amount weight.

I never really believed that the things that I thought about ever really mattered. My silly concepts and morals had always been, even in my own mind, ones that underwent dismissal almost instantly. I felt a deeper connection to you, even still when it had just only been a first impression. I acted the way I did around you for a reason, and since the feelings that I am provided with in your presence are the most intoxicating to the senses, I for the first time in my life experienced a moment where I was not able to think clearly. Simply put, to be in your presence was indubitably the most refreshing thing I have ever had the pleasure of experiencing. Even today it is a feeling that I still believe to be worth noting.

I guess I believe in the power of the human spirit's ability to know that one acts the way that they do for a reason. People in general, act the way they want to, or in a way that pleases them. If that then means everyone is different and unique, then let such a fact be known also.

Eyes

It comes as no secret really to say that there is something beheld in the eyes. I mean to say that when looking into one's eyes, something can be seen Some sort of emotion or calling. To most, the eyes are known as the windows to the soul. To say this, I think not of it as a concept that is completely invalid, but I do however, find little proof that it is actually the soul in which the eyes give way to. It is interesting to think about because the eyes alone can present a lifetime of many different emotions. From happiness expressed in one's lovely crow's feet around the eyes to the tears they wear when become stuck in perpetual sadness, the eyes truly do hold the key to a part of our bodies that isn't just beautiful, but one that is also as deep as the souls in which they embody.

The gift of vision is one that I am, even in this unlucky life, blessed enough to have. In staring deep into the eyes of another I have seen many different types of reflections. In saying this, I mean that there is much that can be said about the eyes, and there is much that the eyes can say. In my eyes for example, there is a certain sense of life and wonder that I myself, have yet to come to explain. It is a small glimmer, a twinkle if you will. A passion for something, a longing of happiness, or of hope. I know it is present for it is the reflection that stares back at me every time I gaze into a mirror. Even when sadness finds me, in the darkest of hours, my eyes seem to expel hope. Even when I feel as though there is no one or anything that can bring me back from the brink, when I am utterly and completely destroyed from the events that I deem now to be ones that were life altering, I keep holding on. Sometimes, it makes me so vexed to think about this glimmer, to think about what it might potentially mean. If it is in fact an expression of my soul, I wonder exactly about what it is expressing. What am I hoping for? If there is hope in my gaze, then how did it come to be there? I feel as though I knew the answer. It was somewhere deep, locked in a part of me that was, at least for now, not willing to give any insight. I do believe however, that one day it might. For, I can only hope.

In general I believe the eyes to be a reflection of the person that is inside. Now whether or not that makes any sense to the sound mind, I am not sure of. If I could elaborate, I would. The only fact that I can say about what the inner being may be is that the one that lives inside of me is one of grace, beauty, and soundness. It is one of tranquility and of subtle ambiguity. It is for certain also, that it is one of age. It is simply in my actions that I can tell this. I can tell in the differences between the manner in which I choose to execute my daily life compared to others. It is simply a sense that I have about myself in comparison to my surroundings, of course.

Having said all of this, it makes me shutter almost, to think about how true and solid all the evidence points to the eyes harbouring the glances of one's soul. For it is not through the warm comfort of my own that I have come to such a conclusion, but rather, it is in the stare of Vergil.

I saw so much in my own eyes, and it pained me to say what I saw in his. Although he was a man of great depth and humility, his eyes bore only the absence of any emotion. His stare was simply cold. Empty. He had no hope, no warmth in his being to fill his mind with thoughts of eventual happiness. His stare beheld nothing of the sort. It was not one of negative affect however. No, not at all. It was simply one that bore no meaning. There was a point in time where our eyes had locked for quite a lengthy period of time and it was then that I did get the best chance at finding any sort of shredded emotion in his eyes, yet I did not. It might have been this moment in time that my worry began to start. Also, I never pondered the concept of what one's eyes might have meant until I saw such a lack of anything in his. It was not disturbing, but rather quite unnerving. He did not have a soul for his eyes to be the windows for.

I stared at him, the whole time, with hope and wonder. I was simply amazed. How could one live life without a soul? I tried to imagine what life would be like if I had not the capacity to love, hope, or feel. Not only that, but I tried also to imagine living in such a condition day after day, without the ability to bring oneself up from the downs and down from the ups. To be constantly flat, in one perpetual state. To be soulless. I went back to that moment on the bridge. I thought to myself that in times of desperation, it would be better to feel nothing than to feel a drowning sadness.

However, it is only in sadness that one can know true happiness, and so, to be sad is only a natural part of the cycle. Vergil had lost his soul. This had always been clear to me; that it was simply the hard truth. I have only ever been as sad as that night on the bridge when I try to think of the situation that he might have been put into that would have caused him to feel such agony, to the point where his only option was to take his own life. To feel a level of pain so high that one can only ever imagine never feeling at all. My love, how I would give you half of my soul if I could but we know both that such an action already took place long ago. For if you had the ability to see what everyone else has seen in my gaze, you would know this to be true also. I sigh in knowing that most likely nothing was seen in my eyes by yours. I have only the ability to however, see the hope that lies at the end of our journey. The hope that a day might exist where I gaze into your eyes and see your soul matching mine in its longing for life.

I believe, with all my heart, that you, Vergil are not forever lost. There is always a way for one to find something that was lost long ago. Sometimes it takes more work to uncover, but even so, this does not mean that it does not deserve to be done. I believe that if anyone could ever be deemed as deserving of any sort of kindness like this, it would be you. You have changed my life, I know, more than once. If I can owe you anything, please let it be a favour such as this. For to have one's soul is the first step in finding one's soul mate and within the absence of yours, only the knowledge of its existence once upon a time can remain. I wish only that I may ferment the idea that one day, and our souls may successfully be together once more.

The basis of my knowledge centers around a certain fact that I wish was not true. There was something about Vergil's eyes that mine did not like. It was not that he was intimidating, even though he was. No, it was rather that I had only the ability to lie to him if I was looking at him straight in the eyes. The first time this occurred I brushed it off and merely believed it to be a reflection of me. That for in some small detail I had developed the ability to present even the opposite from the truth to a person was not something that I believed to have been significant until the second time it occurred.

When it happened again, the circumstances residing around the lie were much different, and I understood it then as exactly what it was. I had only the ability to lie to Vergil's eyes because he did not have anything there that could have detected whether or not it was in fact a lie. Even when I had attempted to tell him that I loved him, I looked him straight in the eyes and could not bring myself to do so. It was as though his eyes prevented me from doing so. The second time it happened, I was so certain that I would have been able to look him straight in the eyes and tell him that I loved him. This was not the case though, I had only the ability to look him in the eyes and lie to him if I chose to speak at all. Given that there were moments where we had starred into each other's eyes without having said any words, but never was there a time where I had been able to tell the truth that I wanted to while looking him in the eyes. It was this only that I did not enjoy about the whole situation. No matter how much I wanted to, no matter how much I wished to, I don't know if ever I would have had the ability to tell him exactly how much I loved him.

These feelings scared me not because they were not true but because I understood very well that Vergil did not have a soul. That was as simple and as plain as it was. He didn't have a soul to be someone's mate with. That was the stage of our love that this life was meant to be. The stage where I was to find him and in turn, get it back for him. This was what scared me the most. That it was true love, my true love.

Often it still sends shivers up my spine when I think about the emptiness that stared back into my determined souls eyes. To realize that one's soul mate has lost his soul to the Devil on a mere technicality is to say, no fun thing. It was however, a thing in which I did know from the start. I never doubted for a second, the fact that this man had not a soul to begin with. He didn't. Not only to me, but also to everyone whom might have had the pleasure of encountering him in their lives knew this to be a true fact. More than anything it was simply a character trait about him. He was a very cold and volatile man. His emptiness seemed to carry father than the deepest waters of all oceans, even of the continents we have not come to discover, and If I may be so bold, the universe in which we reside. When inflicted upon another, it was unsettling to say the least.

This remains one of the reasons why the task that I was bound to finish was so vexing, so daunting. To get ones soul back from the Devil was the most terrifying, yet impulsive thing I have ever set out to do. It seemed almost imperative, as though it was not an option. I would do anything for Vergil, I would even die for him if it meant that he would be eternally happy. All I know is that when I looked into his eyes I saw the depths of Hell; the ice of a man who had gone a long time without his soul. He was empty.

Unable to feel emotion, yet with me he understood it. This I know meant something. It was a different kind of love, and for this, I am certain that too it is understood who the other half of his soul really belongs to. It belongs to me. Not only is the keeping of his soul by the Devil impairing any sort of love and emotion from Vergil, but also, it is keeping my soul here on this earth, still, unable to fulfill its purpose and rest happily until the end of time. Simply because his soul and mine were once one, this means that naturally, the other half of the soul belonged to me, just as my half equally belonged to him. It was never his to loose, and therefore, the contract is nullified.

Dialogue

It had been a night of festivities and celebration for us all. The arrival of a new life, I'd like to believe at least, is always an occasion meriting the utmost level of joy. Of course the arrival of this new life was no exception to this. The mother had been showered with the greatest quality of gifts and the company which she held that night had ensured it to be the most extravagant of times.

It was of course also a time that had been spent, almost in its entirety, with spirits. Everyone except the one expecting, of course, had been enjoying many a drink. Before the night had come to an end, I believe that there had been more than ten different bottles of hard liquor that had been consumed by a party of merely twelve! Of course I had been no different than all the others who decided to partake in these festivities despite the many different ailments I had, who was I to refuse a drink?

Up until the day before it had been uncertain whether or not Vergil was to attend the event. Everyone had it set in their minds that he had chosen to take the easier route and evade all contact with the party members. However, being a member of cet party myself, I had somehow convinced him that night to attend the party. As much as I'd prefer to believe that I had something to do with convincing him to go, it was explained to me at a later date that he had surfaced because of other third party reasons. So the truth, as far as I have come to know presently, remained that I had had no effect on convincing Vergil to go to this party, even if at the time, I thought I had. Not only has the realization of this come to destroy a small part of my soul, but it has also come to confuse most thoughts that I had been once sure about. I guess I wanted to believe that I had meant something to Vergil. That my opinion had matter to him, and since I believed that his presence at the party was the right option, so it was to be done. I had hoped that after the events that had taken place that night; that the only option was to believe that it was true. I wished not to feed my anxieties any longer, for every time I did, they made only more sense to me.

The day had been filled with many different activities, all of which both Vergil and I participated in. I tried to be a companion of sorts for him, for having had the conversation that we did the night before; I understood his anxieties to have been on edge that day also. They say that a picture not only captures the soul that it portrays but also that it captures the moment in which it was taken. I believe for certain, based on this fact, that I did something, that something happened during the day that facilitated the events of the evening. Every photo spoke to me, and as I looked into the eyes of the others, who seemed to go in the direction of the action in which they were focusing on at that time, his eyes seemed to have met those of my camera lens every time. Even when he had not been the main focus of the picture that I was taking, he had been looking over his shoulder, around the corner, at me. I was somewhat flattered to have been the object of his attentions, for I had never really captured the attention of anyone of the opposite sex quite as I had that night in his eyes.

When the evening began, I was amongst those that had been deemed old enough to be given the option of consuming alcohol. Not to say that I was one to do so, but on this occasion, it felt as though it was right to have indulged in a few spirited drinks. Personally, I did not fancy the taste of alcohol; every sip made me shiver or twitch quite a significant bit. As always, the first drink had always been the hardest to swallow. As we indulged in the second, and the third, and the fourth, the night seemed to fade away in the coolness of the summer. It seemed as though one large and exciting blur of a time that no amount of spirits could or would ever allow me to forget, was what that night was meant to be.

At first, the evening had been set to come to a premature end, of course because all of the sprits had been consumed. There had been nothing left to do, nothing left to converse about, and so it seemed that the only option that remained was for everybody to take their leave. That was of course, until the old man showed up. I have never been a fan of the wisdom and diabolical nature that the mind of an old man comes to reach with great age as a generality. And this old man had been no exception to these feelings that began to instil in me naturally upon his arrival. He had with him a bottle of spirits that he had fabricated in his bathtub using peaches that previous summer.

Of what can be said of the old man I cannot really concretely say, for I had known him only for a small fraction of time, and had only spoken a few words to him. But from what I gathered, he had been quite the sad figure in the late years of his life indeed. His wife of forty years had recently passed away, and he found himself carrying all of the burdens of heart he had hoped that she would never have had to do in his passing. He sat now, amongst us, his new friends, with a bottle of these fine spirits and hoped that for a moment, he may find himself happy again. I appreciated this aspect of his character to say the least. I cannot commend the action of giving the sprits he had to the people he did, for I was one of them. It might be plausible for me to say, that this had been the strongest sprit of the whole all night. As it slid down my throat I felt it burn my insides, which stung at each and every gulp. It was certain that in giving this drink to Vergil, I, and all the others amongst us, that the old man had fulfilled his dreams of hoping to fit in with us. He had in a strange sort of way, bought our kind thoughts and good company.

I remember a moment, shortly after we had consumed the last of the bottle, between Vergil and I that had occurred at the dinner table we had all been sitting around, meaning that there had been an audience present. It started off first with a simple, innocent exchange of the feet. Vergil's foot had rubbed against mine, and I had thought nothing of it, and had simply moved my foot a bit closer to myself, thinking that it was my fault that I had been too close to him, and in moving his foot to a different location, he had hit me. As I moved my foot away, there was a small whisper in my soul that hoped it had not been a mistake. I wished that it had been an intentional brush, and that it was Vergil's first attempt to get close to me. Of course, I made sure to apologize to him as I moved my foot. Somehow, someway, there had been something preventing me from moving my foot away, and I knew now, exactly what it had been. It was Vergil's foot, and it had been made clear to me, that the initial brush had been intentional, and that it was his wish to play a game under the table.

Excitement had long filled every inch of my bloodstream, yet I still managed to keep my calm to some extent. I was determined more than anything, to make this game count, for it was ultimately, my one chance at showing Vergil that I was worthy of his magnificence. And so it began. I was shy at first; I had never played these sorts of games before after all. I brought my foot up against his leg and slowly brought it up to his knee. I think he night have enjoyed that segment of my movements a bit too much because before I knew it, his response had been to hook my leg under his and pin it up to the ceiling of the table. He had used such force, that not only had I intensely felt his leg lift mine up against the wood, but the rest of the party sitting at the table who upon until this point had been unsuspecting of our little game. They heard the noise the that bang had made and asked if everything was alright. To keep the pain at bay, I placed my hand over my mouth, and simply nodded that everything was indeed, fine.

He enjoyed my attempts at covering it all up more than I had anticipated he would have. I glanced over to him, keeping in mind that my leg had still been pinned up against the underside of the table, only to witness a devilishly slick smile of satisfaction posted on his lips. His eyes gleamed like a snake that had cornered its prey successfully into the corner that provided no options for escape. The only problem was, as I remained completely calm and collected on the surface, my inside thrilled with the concept of seeing Vergil like this, satisfied. Nothing could have made me happier at this point. There was nothing that made me happier than to willingly have been the small helpless mouse that had no escape from his powerful clutches. I suppose it is more a reflection of me than of him, for the prey is usually not willing at all in its entrapment, but I was however, the most enthusiastic. I cannot speak on behalf of Vergil, but I can certainly say that in one glance of his face, he had noticed me perceiving exactly how content he was. He was now determined to see me crack. To see my face posting the expressions of feelings that I had been having inside. He felt it. He felt the pain that I was enjoying so much at that point. He forced my leg up against the table even harder. I believed my knee to have been fully dislocated, or at least it felt as though quite the forceful push against the wood had been inflicted. Again, I bit my bottom lip and remained persistent. I was very dedicated to not let him win this battle. I was committed to retaining my composure, to not letting him get to me as he had gotten to so many others with his sheer force. At least, not in front of others. If anything was to happen, it was not going to be in front of these strangers, whom I had not known for more than a day in my life.

I had forgotten about my other leg. I realized that it had not been immobilized by Vergil and that it might now serve as a tool for helping the other one escape. It was to be a sneak attack. I decided to take the saucy route and run my other leg up along the inside of his upper thigh. Vergil had not been expecting that for, almost instantly he had released my other leg and a hint of shock overcame his sense of satisfaction. The sense of satisfaction that had faded from his expression had now been all too present on my face. He had believed me to have given up so easily, to have gracefully accepted defeat. As much as it had satisfied me to see him satisfied, I was not one to give up so easily. I was a worthy opponent, and was having far too much fun with this game to have finished it so prematurely.

After I felt as though both of my legs had been completely reinstated to their proper level of function, I decided to retract myself from Vergil and the table all together. Another action of mine that he did not expect. After all, if I was to do anything, it was to keep him on his toes; to keep him interested in me. I stood up, and along with the help of another few nameless individuals, began to dance. We played some music on a nearby stereo and all started to dance around the table. It was not the most professional means of dance, but it was nonetheless dance that was being enjoyed in drunken fun. To move one's body to music, especially when under the influence is, at least I believe, one of the most freeing feelings to be had in the world. I have always been one to dance when any sort of suitable occasion arises. Even when I am waiting to cross the street, if the tune is fitting, I find myself dancing in place as I wait. The freedom of expression that comes along with dance is one that I have always appreciated. Any feeling can be expressed in dance; the human element of it allows it to be so. As I danced around the table completely carefree, I forgot, only for a moment, that there had been others present at the table. I had even forgotten about Vergil in this one moment. I believed that he had noticed the feelings I was putting into my dance for not soon long after I had started dancing, he got up out of his place around the table and had decided to join me also. It was only for a few seconds in which he had attempted to dance. It did not surprise me to see that his intoxication had reached the point where he had finally given way to his animalistic instincts and could no longer do anything except go after the prey in front of him. He grabbed a hold of me and put his arm around my neck and he positioned himself behind me. His arm did not go tightly around my neck for he was a much larger being than I was which made his grip only restrictive enough to have been considered as some type of collar, a form of entitlement essentially.

The others around the table recognized this to be an action of some concern for they started relaying that it was getting late and that it was about time to be getting everyone home. Still with his arm around my neck, we discussed the possibility of all going back to the house of one of the other guests for a sort of afterglow. The elders of the group decided for us that the best option was to simply bring everybody back to their homes.

Vergil pulled me into the car. I had been playing the role of the unsuspecting female. I pretended to think that I did not know what was coming next. At first, I really did believe that we were all going to be dropped off at the house of the party member who wanted to continue the celebration. However, when the car came to its first stop, it had been in front of Vergil's house. He got out of the car, and took a step or two away from it. My heart had dropped into the floors of the seats. It was over. He had seized to want me and I had failed in keeping the interest going until the conclusion of the night. I felt as though I had failed at everything and that I had only myself to blame for feeling the way I did about him in the first place. My stupidity, my idiocracy. My only mistake really being that I felt as though I had even had a chance in the beginning. What a fool I was.

He turned around to close the door of the car. As his arm reached out for the handle I looked at him in sadness, I had hoped that there would have been something more than just this simple ending. Just then, as our eyes met in the shadows of the night, I noticed that he had that smirk of satisfaction plastered on his face once more. My heart immediately began to beat intensely. He grabbed the center of my shirt and pulled me out of the van. With his other hand still on the handle of the door he slammed it shut right as he pulled me out. The night was not over. For us, it had come to just begin.

We had just barely made it up the front steps of his place and through the door when we started to kiss. In a drunken stupor it seemed to be quite awkward; the affection was sort of all over the place. I did not mind for I too was inebriated and was way too excited that my reality had finally intertwined with my wildest dreams. It took a bit of coordination on our parts, but we successfully managed to make it up to the flight of the stairs to his bedroom. The door swung open, and still on top of each other, we entered into the darkness. At first I had no concept of how these affairs of romance were all supposed to unfold, but for some reason, I had always imagined them as ones that would have unfolded in a lighted environment. It never crossed my mind that darkness was the shade of choice for enjoying one another. Down we went. I started to laugh; we had missed the bed, and were now on the floor. I am quite certain also, that in the process, I had knocked over a lamp off of the coffee table and broke it. Luckily, it had been out of the way, and the broken pieces did not interfere with us.

"I want to be my best for you," were the first words that had come out of Vergil's mouth for at least the past few hours. I had been so caught up in kissing him at first that I did not understand the basis in which he had said those words and replied simply with; "What?" "Are you a really a virgin?" He asked me. It made more sense to me now why he wanted to be his best. I had not thought of it like that. It was sweet that he wanted to give me the best time that he could, and I believed that he would do just that. That was the whole reason why I had come so willingly with him, why I had not fought back all of his advances. I wanted to be there with him as much as he did with me. "Yes, I am." I happily replied. It made me more than happy to give myself to him. I believed that if anyone could have benefited from being with me, it might have been Vergil. He had known so much pain, so much heartache. It was time for him to give reason to why he had felt all these feelings before. I knew this time would be different, he knew this time would be different. I would never have dared to do anything to hurt him, or cause him to feel pain the way that all of the females in his past had.

This had been, of course, my initial reaction. Presently, as this was in the past, not a day has gone by where I have not wished that I had lied that night. I wished more than anything that I had lied to Vergil and told him that I had not been a virgin. I cannot say whether or not it would have made a difference, for I took the route that I was meant to take, the route of honesty. I wished that I had not been honest that night. I wished that I had the ability to have lied to Vergil, to have been everything that he wanted me to be. I thought that it was a good thing that I had not had any sort of romance with anyone before; I believed that this was what gave me an edge on the other girls. I was new and shiny, and had all the naiveté that a virgin might be supposed to have. I thought he would have been happy to have been the first man that I had ever loved. I must not know much, for all I had thought had been just that, thoughts.

Up until this point he had been on top of me, and it crossed my mind that this was not how I imagined my first time to have been. Well, not indefinitely at least. I had imagined there to have been somewhat an equal exchange of being on top and on bottom. You know, to get the full experience. Quite stupidly, I asked him "Why are you on top?" He got off of me and went somewhere in the darkness. I heard a bit of shuffling, but that was all I heard really. "Okay, get on the bed." He said to me as a shadowy character standing in the corner of the room. I did exactly as he said. The bed had not been far off, so I simply grabbed a hold of it and pulled myself up onto it.

For a moment I had begun to wonder about all the other girls that must have been in this bed at one point or another in time. I knew in a way, I had been different from them, because none of them had never had sex before. As I waited for him to re-emerge from the darkness, and for the rustling to stop, a sense of tragedy came over me. Vergil had been with so many other women before now, and even though I might have felt special in that moment, during that night, the sharp reality was that I was not. He had done this before so many times, and I was only a number to him.

It was strange that I found myself not caring even if this had been the most likely option. It seemed again that my anxieties had simply been giving way to the worst possible reasoning to the situation. Yes, I was completely aware that these types of actions were nothing new for Vergil, but they were for me. Simply put, I guess it didn't really matter that they were not new for him, for if they were new enough to me, the experience, being a shared one, would have been different. That was at least the logic that ran through my mind that night.

It took a few moments but he joined me on the bed. He had started back up with the aggression, which I had come to love so much. In between the breaths that I had been allotted when he did not have his tongue in my mouth hand and his hand around my throat, I made sure to moan and groan. Ensuring, of course, that I was properly expressing all of the pleasure that I was now receiving from him also.

All of a sudden he decided to get off of me. He pulled away from me in the swiftest fashion and backed away to the other side of the bed as far as he could. I instantly thought that I had done something wrong. That I had gotten this far, and at last, his sobriety had kicked in and he realized exactly just how repulsive I had actually been. I laid there for a few seconds, in complete shock. I was initially, quite upset. I did not say anything. I simply decided to get up and leave. As I got up off of the bed, Vergil had started to make some sort of noise. Before I knew it, he had thrown up all over his bed.

As if I had not been upset enough already for being disgusting and repulsive to him, it had to be fermented concretely in vomit. I have never really had any sort of luck however, that might have led to me believing that the unfolding of these events would have been anything less than normal. I think it is more likely that Vergil's level of intoxication had reached the point of expulsion. As much as I want to believe that this is what happened, the timing does not supports its case. There had been at least half an hour that had elapsed since the last of his drinks had been consumed. Was it possible, even after that sort of time lapse, to purge? I was not completely sure. It may have been a combination of the two. Perhaps my repulsion mixed with his intoxication resulted in a combination that was not to be handled by his stomach. I am not sure, and I believe that there is a good chance that I might never be either.

The submissive side of me had kicked in somewhat, and of course I offered to help him and saw if there was anything that I could have done. "Did you want a glass of water?" I asked him in the most inconsiderate of tones. I wished now that I had not been as snarky in my offered assistance but it had been quite hard for me to even try and understand the magnitude of what had just happened. Ultimately, I was upset. I genuinely believed that this night would have taken a turn for the better, and now, I stared only into the face of disgust. He mumbled something under the pile of vomit he laid in now. I did not listen because there really was no reason for me to have done so. The whole situation had just been wrong. Everything had gone wrong, and if there had ever been an image of how it must have felt to have given yourself to someone special, it certainly was not this.

Untitled

He got up. "Wait." Was the only order I received as he left the room in a hurry. Wait. He was telling me to wait. For what? It was done. It was over with. There really was no reason for me to stay any longer. I didn't know where he left his room to go, and at that point I really did not care. I had an image of what this night was supposed to be like in my mind, and this simply was not it. I had only the will to leave these unfavourable circumstances behind and get on my way. Of course, I obeyed the command he barked. As much as I had not wanted to, there was a small part of me that felt as though it had to. So I waited in the darkness, as the smell of fresh vomit filled the air around me. There was nothing poetic that existed in this moment; there was only a sense of uninterrupted disappointment that filled my existence.

After a few moments he came back. While he was away I had heard the toilet flush so I understood him to have been in the bathroom for what might have been another round of purging. I didn't really care anymore, not just about everything that had gone wrong, but also about anything really. What he was doing in the bathroom had nothing to do with me and I felt as though the time that I had passed here in this room was over, and the only sensible action left to be done was to take my leave. And perhaps also, to never return. I wanted to just leave. Just leave the whole thing behind and wish that I had the ability to make it all go away. It had been embarrassing and memorable enough to know that such wants would never transfer into reality. I wanted nothing to do with any of these affairs anymore. That night was the one chance that was to be had between us and it had clearly been blown up into pieces. Now, whether or not there was some reason why it had all unfolded this way, I had yet to become aware of.

As I sat there on the floor like a hopeless child that had lost their parents, all of my feelings became put on hold as Vergil barged back into the room. Without saying a word, once again, he grabbed me by the clothes on my chest and took me out of the room. He brought me into the bathroom and threw me against the wall. I cannot say that at this point I had been into these shenanigans as I had been the first time around. The tone had changed from sultry to pathetic and my passion for it all had faded. I wanted to have a passionate evening with Vergil and he vomited all over the picture I had painted in my head.

He pinned me up against the wall with his hand more violently than the last time. It knocked some sense into me and almost instantly, I became interested again. As he slowly kissed my neck, he made his way aggressively back up to my lips. This was the part that I loved, the feeling of being helpless as he took my clothes off wearing that ever so expressive smile of satisfaction on his face. I tried to ask myself exactly why it was that I had any my clothes on still at all. As no answer surfaced upon the shores of my mind, I realized that it didn't matter since I no longer had any of my clothes on, so the question was redundant. I wanted to reach out and attempt to take his clothes off also. It seemed like the logical counter reaction to the action of him taking mine off, but that never happened. As I reached my hand out, Vergil grabbed a hold of his clothes first and began to take them off in a hurry. Undertones of disappointment filled into my mind. I wanted to take his clothes off; to per se feel what might have been waiting for me underneath it all. I was excited to be excited for the first time. The clothes were coming off, and with the contact of his skin on mine, the picture in my mind began to clear.

He took his hand away from my neck and used it to turn the shower on. He stepped into the shower and pulled me in with him with his other hand. "Oh Vergil, it's so hot." I almost wailed. The temperature of the water had actually been quite scolding. He let go of me and went to put his hand on the faucet to adjust the temperature. I pushed his hand away. "No, I like it." Almost instantly again, his hands held me up against the wall. "I want you so bad; I'm ready." His hands had been so tight around my neck this time that the words came out as almost a whisper. "Tell me." He said very firmly. He loosed his grip slightly to let me speak more fluently, an action that was definitely appreciated. I didn't really have anything to say, or anything to tell him. I did not really know anything about love or expressing it, I had never been put in any sort of situation prompting me to do so before. In that moment, I had no words to speak. I remained master only of the words in which I had not spoken that night. I had wished I could have said something, anything to have made him think of me the way the thought about other females.

He waited a few seconds for a response from me, and after it had been realized that it was to never have come, his aggression increased. For the first time that night, he sunk his teeth deep into the skin tissue of my neck. I let out the loudest scream of satisfaction. Never had anyone done anything like that to me before. The pain, the level of feeling that he had inflicted, were all absolutely fantastic. "Please don't bite me again; I love the feeling of it too much." Still wearing the smirk that he had been all night, he bit me again, even harder this time, on the shoulder. I let out another inconsolable scream of acceptance. Senses of warmth filled my entire body. I was not sure how much longer I would be able to take the level of seduction he was playing out now. I had wanted him so badly. Surely he also knew this by now. I was whimpering and wailing at every touch. After a few more intense moves, he slowly moved his hand down and put his fingers inside of me. At first just one, and as I moaned, another.

"I wish I could have that." he expressed. It was at this time that utter confusion set into my brain. I did not understand. What did he mean? His will was to be done. He needn't wish any longer. I was here; the moment was here. No level of circumstances more perfect than these would ever arise again. As he shook his head in amazement, he withdrew his hand and backed away from me. "What?" I asked like a confused sad puppy dog. "I don't think you understand the level of restraint I have right now." was the response that Vergil had decided to answer my question with. I did not understand his process of thinking. I had wanted all of this. I had wanted every single aspect of this moment, and now I was expected to come to the understanding that nothing was to transpire? "I don't understand why you have any, you don't need it." I started to snap back. This had been one emotional roller coaster, and I was not having any of it anymore. This had been the second instance of what I would consider to be rejection. It hurt just as much as the first time and now I was the only one to blame for its happening. "Get on your knees." He barked another command. Of course I obeyed.

Even after making me feel repulsive for a second time, his will became done. I got on my knees and knew exactly what was expected of me in that position. Coincidentally it happened to be exactly what I had desired to do anyways. I tried to get as much of him as I could in my mouth because he tasted so great. Before I had even the slightest moment to attempt to lick his dirty member clean, it was over. As I looked up he opened his mouth and said "Okay, get up." As I withdrew, he grabbed my wrists and pulled me up. Even standing up, I couldn't help myself to do anything else but center my eyes downwards and look at him. Vergil came to stand right up and close next to me and wrapped his arms around me tightly. I could not bring myself to return his embalming hug. "That's just not you." He sobbed.

"We can be close." He sobbed. "We can be as close as you want to be, I just can't do that to you." He couldn't even say the word sex in front of me now, and I am certain that sobriety came to hit him in the face. I had no emotions left to give him. Not to say that I had been cold, but rather that I did not have any sort of response to give. I genuinely did not understand what was happening. I instantly thought that I had been wrong, that I was just unattractive. Instantly my mind came to such conclusions as this. I blame myself constantly for a great deal of issues which may or may not actually deserve blame. That was and will always be simply how I have always been. "I have never had anything like this before. You have a gift, you're special. My virginity was taken from me, and I can't do the same to you. I love you, but I don't trust you." He hugged me with more emotion than any other action I had felt all night, and as he began to cry he looked me straight in the eyes and pleaded, "Hug me." As much as I wanted to return his passion, I could not. He withdrew himself from me and sat down. He pulled me down with him by my arms once more.

I sat there in the bathtub with the hot water hitting my back, and my face became expressionless. I gently leaned over to the wall and placed my head on it and simply stared over Vergil's shoulder at the wall behind him. This man. Emotionally, I had nothing left to give him. Nothing I could have said would have allotted his mind to change. All of my hopes and dreams washed down the drain, and my mind resembled the chipped off paint spots now facing me. I felt smaller than a particle, with a worth measuring even less than that. I resented Vergil in that moment for making a big deal of what I knew to have been a factor that was not his to do so with. It was all supposed to mean nothing. This night. It had been meant simply to have been a fraction of my being, nothing that would have been anything significant in either my life or his. It was in not taking advantage of the situation that had presented itself to him that brought it to mean something much more. I had meant something to him. The only girl that Vergil had not ever had sex with. If the other of the two options that night would have transpired, he would have been right, it would have meant nothing. I would have been just another female, another betrayer. Now this, this was significant. "You have to find someone like me, someone special like me who understands."

The nonsense that he began uttering now was uprooting. I suspected that his anxieties surpassed even mine in their constructions. He believed that there had been other options besides him, and that it was now my duty to find someone special that was like him, yet, was not to be him. No one that I have ever been interested in has ever come to show a return of interest in me, so I did not understand why I thought that Vergil would have been any different. As I opened my mouth to try and refute such ideas, he put his hands over it, holding it shut, which did not allow such folly to occur. The truth was that I did not want to be with another person, I only wanted him. He had only ever been the one. He had always only ever been the only one.

I wanted to tell him exactly how much he meant to me, but I know it would have scared him and he would have surely taken to distancing himself from me. I dreaded the thought of my life without him. It made my soul upset to think that Vergil did not think of himself as special. He was the most beautiful, most fantastic man I had ever known in my life. I dare to say also that he shall remain all of those things and more until the end of it. He was deserving of me, and I wished that I would have been able to persuade him into thinking the same thing.

"Say something." He barked another order. I had nothing to say. Nothing that I could have said would have made him change his mind about his feelings for me, as I found speaking to be of no use. I did not understand why he had even wanted me to say anything. I had nothing in this moment. Even he could tell such notions within the soul that was not present in my disposition now. Something happened that night in the bathtub. As my head lay against the tiles on the wall, I felt empty for the first time in my life. As though nothing in my life mattered anymore. I am certain that if during this time, if my life would have come to an end, I would not have been upset in the least by it. I had lost the will to function as myself. Clearly being myself had brought me into the dreadful situation that I was in now, and so I was of no use. Even Vergil understood that. I did not say anything. If anything, my silence spoke enough. "Well then, I guess were done here. Wait." He spoke as he got up and turned the water off. He grabbed a towel and dried himself off as I sat still with my head against the wall in perpetual shock. He left the room and I did not take much notice of his absence. He returned with a towel for me and I dried myself off also. He gave me a change of clothes and we went back into his room. The air had now completely been filled with the scent of his fresh vomit as it began to fester into the mattress.

We laid down on the floor together, and for the last time, he grabbed me and held me tight. This time I tried now to refuse. The last memory of this night was dreadful. Caressed in the arms of a man that I had not the slightest will to be caressed by in that moment. The last object I had not been given a choice on was one that did not fare me well. All he wanted was to caress me, to hug me. Emotional abuse is much worse than physical. For if one attacks the mind, the body and the soul go with it, for they all go hand in hand. All that night had been for me was emotional abuse. I hated that Vergil had taken me on this roller coaster and ended it only in emotion. I did not want any feelings that he had to offer me. I wanted to feel what love was like, and instead I felt only sadness and pain that I had not been enough for him. He fell asleep with his teddy bear, who in that night, was not able to do the same.

Aftermath

I had so many questions that I could not find answers for. I woke up the next morning with the biggest smile posted on my face and the most overbearing sense of sorrow resonating in my heart. At this point I didn't even know what I wished for. I was a level of confused that had surpassed refreshing long ago. I was sore and covered in bruises and bite marks and had spent the night being tightly caressed by the man that I considered to have been completely suitable of having me, but yet was still a virgin. Perhaps I was more upset with myself than anything else. I'm sure that if the circumstances were different, if the factors that kept Vergil from wanting to have sex with me had not been present, then such a want might have successfully established itself as a need.

That didn't help the fact that all I could think about was what had happened last night between us. I tried really hard to forget on the walk home, to try imagine it as all having been just a dream. I was too smart for that, and my tiny unknowing pussy was all too wet for that now. It was too late to forget. Vergil felt as though he had done the right thing last night in not having sex with me, when all he did was ferment my wanting of him into a physical need. I did not really want to want him, but my body allowed only for the opposite to be true. Even now, the morning after, I was still so wet and wanting of him. This may have been actually due to his rejecting me, but I know not for certain if it was a feeling all on its own or one that was caused by another.

I was too excited and flustered to do anything else that morning other than take the humble hour long walk back to my home with the hopes of settling all my emotions by the that time I did. This time I passed the bridge without even realizing that I was on it right up until the very last set of benches along the side. I was too entangled in my mind this time to have even allowed any feelings of dread or unconditional darkness to find me. I was busy thinking about Vergil and how absolutely perfect he was, to have even cared about the bridge, let alone the terribly real feelings I have experienced through its presence before. Vergil was all I could think about, and it concerned me that I knew my thoughts to be neither positive nor negative but rather simply present. It was a completely unexacting influx of ideas, emotions, and expressions. As I came to pass the bridge entirely, I stopped and stood at the beginning of the road to try and figure out exactly what emotion I was feeling now, was it a positive one or a negative one?

Without the influence of the bridge in my mind now to alter the results of how to accurately answer this question, I am sure still that how I was actually feeling was still more negative than positive. Sure, I glowed with the smile and light that accompanied everyone in the morning after having an intimate encounter with another, but I felt more or less wrong about how the whole situation unfolded. Seriously, how could it have been that I had managed to allow Vergil to have inflicted so much pain onto my body, yet was actually still a virgin? The fact that I stood in the street now looking like some terribly battered wife, but with a look of serene happiness on my face also might have answered such a question. To be sincerely honest, I did not mid the bruises and marks in the least. In fact, I found them to be kind of sexy. They were a constant reminder of the sheer force and influence this man had over me, like little sticky notes of love. Many may argue such a reality, such actions, as many things but any facet of what love might be considered as. I did not think of it this way. I thought of it as the truest form of love that Vergil had to offer me, if anything. He was in the moment of inflicting them on me, the truest representation of himself; and I appreciated the honesty. Not only that, but to be completely frank, I liked the bruises that I wore now. Vergil did not have much to give me, but in this case, he did.

To say so, more or less otherwise, I might be one of the only people that could possibly have seen anything positive about this situation, but I did. I liked the marks that he made on me that night, and I truly did feel important and loved the entire walk home. If this was the way that he chose to show his love, if it was simply him being himself and acting himself towards me for the first time, then how could I have possibly been justifiably upset with his actions? I couldn't be. I didn't understand the whole situation because if I liked what he was doing, and a point of discussion for him was the fact that I was virgin, why wouldn't he have wanted to make it so that it would no longer have been able to be one? I hated to admit that it might have also been just me and my lack of experience in this field that led Vergil to do what he did.

So it has come to this. To live in a time where it can be considered a negative thing to be a virgin inexperienced in sex. In all of the lives that I have lived, not just the last one spent with Vergil, I do not believe that I would ever have been able to say that I have been part of a generation that valued highly sexualized and aware females over the blissful ignorance of virginity. My shock concerning the whole situation then, might only have surfaced as a result of its presence lacking other times that my soul has embodied a female body on this earth.

He seemed to make a big deal out of something that I did not believe was his to do so with. Was being a virgin really something that was special? Did I really have a gift to give someone or was it just a lie that Vergil told be because he did not want to have sex with someone who would become unconditionally attached to him in doing so? I am sure my anxieties had some input relevant to answering such a question. Maybe Vergil did genuinely love me, which might have been the exact reason why he chose not to have sex with me. Since he was known for his numerous partners and experience, it was special for him to have not done so with me then. Perhaps this was the truest statement that I could have made, but I think it is more likely that Vergil did not want to have sex with me because he did not find me attractive enough to do so. It is not that I mean to call myself ugly or unattractive, because I surely do not think such things about myself, but rather I mean to say that Vergil did not find my virginity attractive. It is through these bases that has led me to conclude it is the truth, for one cannot be held in a negative light through a subject that is being labelled as a gift also.

I wanted to put how I felt in terms that were simpler and more relevant to the time which has labelled me in such a negative fashion. I was embarrassed to be myself. I was a virgin that had never had sex and the one man that I can concretely say I have loved did not want to have sex with me specifically for that reason. Life has made it intentional that I shall never come to poses the capabilities to come to terms with that as a true statement, even though it was the epitome of truth. Was being a virgin truly such a big deal that the only man I have loved and deemed worthy of having me could have been justified in his actions? I wanted to say no. Reality told me that he was simply doing the right thing and that through not having sex with me, was showing me that he cared. Others have told me this also, so I did know it to be true. I wanted to know then, why was it that he cared about me, what was the reasoning? He didn't value anyone else in this respect, so there had to be some reason why he did with me. Even though I was completely unnerved by the fact that he didn't want me, I was appreciative that he was honest with me. It is in his action speaking louder than words though, that I have come to realize now, just how much I wanted him. He was perfect, and I know for certain that I would never find a man as deserving of having me as he was that night.

I was hurt also because in the words that Vergil spoke to me that night, he did not find himself worthy of this gift either, or he simply wanted to throw it back into my face because he truly was a man without a soul. Maybe his rejection proved that he did in fact have a soul, or at least that in rejecting me, he showed that he had the potential to have had one, once upon a time.

It was this whole level of certainty that came to torment me on my walk home that morning. How far could my analysis accurately go? There were so many options of reasoning for why Vergil didn't want me, and I could not narrow down which one it was for they all provided the same level of logic in their answers. It was certain that my soul was not expecting for him to have been the way he was in this life; quite cold yet intensely pensive. I wanted to believe my anxieties had long overthrown the sanity inside my brain, but it occurred to me to think of what might happen if this was all true? If Vergil didn't actually have his half of soul but the Devil did because we met and fell in love in another life and since I remained as the only half of the soul left that had the option of embodying a human, I was the one that could mend our soul back together again. My mind chose quite the fantasy to latch onto, for if it was in fact true, then I had to do this, I had to try with all of my soul to get the other half back. It was not a subject that was so easily dismissible because if I did, if I just threw the whole idea away, Vergil might never get his soul back, and he might never come to live a life with me as one complete soul again.

I am not sure if I would have felt so strongly about him had he taken the route that pandered to my desires last night. It might have been possible for a night of inebriated, steamy, rough, and firm sex to have led me to feel even more so attached to him, but since it did not unfold in this fashion, I cannot conclude upon it. I felt as though it might have made me much more content about the situation, meaning I would have been happier to have executed this whole task of getting his soul back had he been the man that I knew him to be. Either way, I had a contract to hold. I was to try my best to get his soul back, whether or not he recognized who I was and who I had been to him once. If I didn't, my soul would then too be in jeopardy. Even if it was not true, the possibility of failing to do so was what kept me walking down the street smiling as I hugged myself in the warmth of his clothes.

A Reoccurring Dream

What is within the dreams that we have as humans? I have never met a person in my life that has told me that they have never had a dream. Dreams are something that we as humans inexplicably do, sometimes often, and sometimes not. For a while now, I have been trying to understand the possibilities of what a dream could possibly mean. As much as I'd like to say that all of our dreams mean nothing, I cannot. There is nothing more comforting, for example, then waking up from a dream where you had seen a lost relative who assured you that they were okay. That it was okay to let go of them because they are resting in peace. This phenomenon has not occurred to me personally, but it has to a dear acquaintance of mine, and she found much comfort in knowing that the diseased relative in question, whom she had not had a chance to say goodbye to, was resting in peace. Such an occurrence may simply be explained by our subconscious mind. If the subconscious chooses to do so, it might be able to show us certain scenes or images in our dreams to try and tell us the things that it believes we need to hear. At least this explanation can serve as a valid explanation for why she had a dream concerning a death that she did not properly get to say farewell to.

I can't help but disagree with this sort of explanation, no matter how comforting it is. For if the inner workings of the subconscious to serve as the basis for explaining why we see what we do when we dream, I am prompted then, to severely question my existence in this world, and what I was truly meant to do. Certainly, if I can rest assured of anything, it is that I do not have the dreams of what any one person would define as a normal. Although it has never been in my taste to be like anyone else, I awaken most nights from my slumbers in absolute terror and fear; an aspect of my existence that I have really come to despise for the vividness presented within these dreams is one that has caused me to break with reality. There have been occurrences where I have not been able to tell whether or not I had been dreaming upon waking up. Death also is no stranger to my dreams, and it seems also that I am the one prescribing such a fate to others present in my dreams, never anyone else unto me. Often, I awake almost to the point of shaking and gasping for air trying to catch my breath, and looking for any sort of proof that the violent death that I have not only just witnessed, but that I have also committed, had only been a figment of my imagination.

Unfortunately for me, these occurrences in which Death is present in my dreams has been a theme for so long that it has become somewhat habitual for me to awaken in a stirred up state, but no longer ever with any fear at the events that had just unfolded. The darkest and most wilted of scenes end at the turn of dawn and even though their tones stay etched in my mind forever, I always awake to find no true relations between my dreams and my real life. Not ever. No family members or close acquaintances can ever be found within my dreams; usually they are people I barely know, if not characters that seem to be pulled completely from the constructs of my mind. I understand this concept about myself; I can only hope that this land of darkness that finds me every night is not the result of my subconscious trying to convey any ideas to me.

As a result of these facts, I have always simply thought that my dreams meant nothing, and it is now my common practice to have somewhat trained myself to become unresponsive to all of these tragedies of night. I guess it might make sense to attribute all of this Death and the shock that comes to me after seeing it as some internal fear of actually dying myself.

It is not that I fear death; rather, it is that I believe that it is completely unjust for my life to have been so intensely shortened compared to the lives of others. Death is not something that a human experiences exclusively as a human. It is the fear of not knowing what comes in the afterlife where most individuals find their quarrel with death. I find mine simply in the fact that I shall come to answer this question much sooner than others.

Nevertheless, every time I dream, I am thankful. I understand fully that not everyone dreams on a nightly basis, and since I do, no matter what type of dream, I am still thankful for the opportunity of escaping this dreaded reality I live in. I simply have understood my dreams as just that, dreams. They have never crossed with reality, so I never really thought of any reason why I dreamt the things that I did. There were never any correlations in ideas, so I never deemed any message to be found within their contents. That is until rather recently, when I had the most interesting dream that I have ever had before in my life. Coincidentally enough, it was not my first time having it either. This time the dream was slightly different though. This time the dream had relevance in my life.

Trying to expand on an idea that is already quite ambiguous surely cannot end in positive results. I hate trying to find some kind of explanation for any of this, and time and time again, I have failed. Dreams are hard enough to try and evaluate, and I fear that by delving into a level deeper on this subject will cause its true meaning to become clouded beyond any logical reasoning or meaning. Something can be found in a dream. I may not ever be able to solidly say what, but to say that there is something to be found within the contents of a dream is one of the most valid conclusions I can make. As I am sure any other human living on this earth can make with me also.

This dream was different in many ways. The first being that it is the only reoccurring dream I have ever had in my life.

There was a woman. She wore only the most beautifully laced items of clothing. Modern of course, but they always had a lovely slightly Victorian tone to them. Her tops would differ quite frequently, sometimes she would be wearing a simple tank top, and others she would have on something as intricate as a satin black whale boned corset accented with frills on both the top and bottom. She was beautiful. The most fantastically classy lady I have ever encountered in my life, either awake or dreaming. Her makeup was always almost perfectly applied, and the soft vampire red curls of her hair bounced as she walked, swaying from one side to the other. The colours of her eyes shimmered always. When her face was hidden amongst the shadows and when light reflected upon it. Her eyeliner as contrasting with her fair pale skin as day and night, and her lips bitten with the deepest shade of red lipstick, was always applied perfectly and never smeared on her teeth. If ever I had been taken aback in awe at a woman, it was in the sight of her. One peculiar thing about this woman was, however, that no matter what season in which she visited me, she always wore a skirt. I must have seen her over fifty times in my life and not once had I ever noticed her wearing a pair of pants. I only ever took notice of this because of the events that might occur in the dream itself also.

In the dream I was never looking at her through the eyes of another person, but through some kind of birds eye view. Not quite completely aerial, but my view was always elevated, and I was looking down at the two people that were involved in this dream. The woman, who could have been no older than twenty, would walk up a set of four stairs to the door of a house. She would stand on the porch, holding a pair of pants. They were usually jeans, and they were always folded neatly into a square. She would take away one of her arms from underneath the pants and ring the doorbell. The pants were always some kind of intricate pattern. They were always very nice looking jeans, but they were also quite large. The person that would answer the door was a younger version of my current self. At the time where I had been having this dream on a regular basis, I was still small, maybe six or seven years old. Since my age in the dream reflected that of my real age in real life, of course the pants were all that much larger for me than they were for the woman that was holding them. I would open the door and say a greeting to the woman, usually hello. She never said anything to me, she would simply smile and place the pants in my hands and then would proceed to turn around and walk down the stairs. Her smile was not one of joy, but one of committing an action as though she knew something that I didn't. It was somewhat of a smirk, but it was filled with knowledge, about something that she knew I did not. I would always stare in confusion, as though I had missed something, some concept in its entirety.

I would stand at the door and watch her walk down the stairs. Once she got to the bottom step I would close the door, with the pants still in my hands, and turn around and walk down a long hallway that had many different doors along it. At the end of the hallway on the right side, was the last door on that strip. All of the doors looked the same; they were all just plain and simple white doors. However, I would walk past all of the other doors, still holding the pants of course, and then open the last door on the right side. It was a closet, like the ones that housed bath towels outside of bathrooms. Except this closet held only pants. Every time I had this dream, another pair of pants got added to the closet. The last time I had this dream, the closet had been filled with pants. The last pair of pants I ever received from the woman had come to complete the stack. Once the closet was full of pants that the woman had given me, I never had that dream again. To be completely honest, I had forgotten about it for quite a solid amount of years. It was the strangest because I had this dream many times when I was a child, but as soon as the closet had been filled with all the pants that the woman had gave me, the dream stopped occurring. It was as though my subconscious put a cap on the dream because there was no more room in the closet. When I was small, for the first few weeks after the closet had filled up, I remember being sad that the tone of my dreams had switched from it, and I had missed seeing the lovely woman who had given me all of these oversized pairs of pants. However, as it so happens to be, I did have this dream one more time.

It came much later on in my life this time. At least ten years later. It seems funny to me to think that it had come during a period in my life where I had completely forgotten about it, right up until I had it once more. It was the point in my life that I could classify as being one where it would have been least likely for me to think about this dream. Isn't that usually how these things happen? Always, when we least expect them, so as to have the greatest impact in our lives.

The dream started off just as it always had. The woman walked up the steps that lead to my porch, holding a pair of oversized embellished pants, and proceeded to ring the doorbell. The child version of me then proceeded to open the door and accept the pants. However this time, she did not close the door or bring the pants to the closet. She simply started lifelessly at the woman, and opened her mouth wanting to utter a word to her. Yet she didn't. She was taken aback this time, at the sight of the woman now. The woman whom I had completely forgotten about until this moment, had me in awe. I was now the little girl and the woman staring back at my confusion was what I looked like now. She was me. She had been me all along. I no longer witnessed this occurrence from a bird's eye point of view; I experienced it this time through the eyes of my childish self. I stood there with my jaw open, attempting to say even one completely formed word to the woman, yet I could not. This time, as I stood at the door watching her walk away, my eyes followed her to a car and a man standing beside it. It did not surprise me to see that the man she was standing next to was you, Vergil. The two hugged and kissed, then proceeded to get into a car and drive away. I stood there still and stiff, with only the capability to look at the two in complete jealousy. Before the woman got into the car she gave me one last assuring wink. It consoled me somewhat, because she was happy. She had succeeded in getting the man she had always desired and now, I stood there with a pair of pants just as I had when I was a child, unable to have the same reality she did.

I woke up from this dream in a state where I didn't actually know what to do. I laid in my bed for at least another hour and starred at the ceiling trying to process what had just happened. It was enough of a shock that I had the dream again to begin with let alone the startling additions that were thrown in the mix this time. I was the woman all along. She looked exactly as I did now, yet there was something different about her. She had something I didn't. Of course, she had Vergil. As much as I'd like to place that to be the startling difference between her and I, I cannot. There was something else, something that I couldn't quite put my finger on. In a way, she seemed to glow. Her smile was real, and she was exuberantly radiant because of it.

I knew what had made her that happy; I simply did not have the courage to say it. It was Vergil. But it was not just his physical presence that made her seem so similar yet so alien to me, it was how she acted as a being that was an extension of him. She was confident in this light and she seemed to love herself, which of course, was more than I could say for myself.

I did not love myself. Even in laying there, trying to understand the depth of what my dream was trying to tell me, all I could think about was how happy she was, how happy Vergil made her. She made it. I wanted to know what her secret was desperately, even after the dream had finished. I wanted to know what she did to get him, how it was possible for her to be with him and not me. And like the little girl with the pants did, I lay there in awe unable to speak a single word or come to any conclusion on what had just happened. I asked myself why this was the time that I didn't shut the door, why had I not just woken up? Why did I have this dream now, at this point in my life? What did it all mean, if anything? I wondered also if the woman had always gone to that car to Vergil, after she gave me the pants. I never really noticed what her actions were as a child, since I had almost instantly shut the door every time. I had to put the pants away. I didn't pay any attention to her once she gave them to me.

It was never up until this point, up until I took on the role of my childish self that I witnessed what she did after the transaction occurred. I had always shut the door behind me, never looking back to see where she went. I wondered how my current situation might have been different had I not shut the door sooner, had I witnessed what the woman did after she gave me the pants. I wished that I had seen her walk to him before I met him. Things might have been different. I might have experienced the dream as the woman I saw leaving with the man I loved as opposed to the small, insignificant, worthless, speechless child that I was, and perhaps, would remain as forever.

As of this moment in time, I have not ever had this dream again. And as every night goes by, filling my mind with countless numbers of meaningless dreams I can only come to the conclusion that having this dream one last time meant something. I'd like to believe that it was someway of my subconscious assuring me that there might still be a possibility of achieving my dream of having the chance to be that happy woman. That all hope was not lost. Having that dream made me so upset and sad that I was not as happy as the woman was, as happy as I could be. Perhaps one day, I can only hope that I will have this dream again. Hopefully if such a night would every meet my fate again, I shall take on the role of the woman whom I have always known to be the most radiant and cheerful of souls. As the woman whom showed in every smile and step that she took, the by-product of being with one's true love and the everlasting effects of achieving such. His presence in her life showed clearly though her soul and disposition. I believe, that in the woman's wink, she was trying to let me know that although I lay now in my bed confused and alone, a day might come where my soul will be given the opportunity to embrace happiness. Of course, happiness cannot be known without being able to concretely define what sorrow is. Every time I think about this, about Vergil, I am overcome with tears of sorrow and sadness. In feeling this way I understand now, that this was the only possible route that could have been taken if I was ever meant to have a chance to achieve true happiness. I have felt every emotion in thinking about this man. It is in such a fact as this, that I have come to know him as the one that would permit my soul to move onto the next stage of happiness and fulfillment. This was something my subconscious knew also.

Necessity

It is difficult for me to differentiate between what is a necessity and what is simply a desire. I think often that this is due to the fact that my lifestyle has simply made the two ideas to have only the smallest level of difference between one another. I have always had difficulties with the difference between what I consider to be a need and what I consider to be a want. It takes a lot of effort and caution for me to even exist, and so things that others might consider to be wants, I have to consider as needs.

A simple example of this is breakfast. I know quite a few people who do not eat breakfast, whether they do not have the time for it, or simply they prefer to eat later in the day. Whatever the reason, I can come to understand it, for I know even myself, some days I really don't even feel as though I want to eat breakfast. I need to however. If I do not eat within two hours of waking up, my body will start to get very upset with me. I will develop physical pains and quite a severe headache. I understand this most likely to be the result of my perpetual poor health, and because of this something that is a want for others has fashioned itself as a need for me.

The example of breakfast was only to serve as a simple example that outlined just how intertwined the lines between necessity and want are for me. It has always been like this. Just as it has always been, it fascinated me to consider Vergil into this equation also. The whole situation had been all too perfect to have done anything else with it. I wondered exactly about that night. I wanted to believe that it did not mean anything; I wanted to believe that it was nothing; that the whole thing could have been as easily dismissed as my need to have breakfast was. It wasn't that simple, it was anything but. I had never experienced anything so perfect to describe my situation of necessity and desire than that of what happened between Vergil and I. I had set out on this journey hoping to find an explanation, to find the perfect love story. To find something, that arguably, did not exist. As much as I had wanted to be with Vergil for the rest of my life, I understood that I don't believe it to ever be possible. The story was, at this point, done. It was finished and quite perfectly so.

Ultimately, Vergil had given me everything that I had ever hoped to achieve in knowing him. As much as I would have loved nothing more than to have made Vergil as happy as he made me, doing so might not have been as perfect and as poetic as this all was. It was necessary for him to have rejected me in the fashion he did, for it was tragic, romantic, and fantastic. It seemed almost surreal to me the way in which I had accepted being his; and yet he felt too damaged to be accepting of my love. What perfection. I'd like to attribute the surrealism of it all to his perfection, but this was not the case. I felt as though truly to have been the love story that it was, it was necessary for him to have rejected me. This whole thing was necessary. It was meant to be, which is the part that scares me the most. I am sure that it was meant to be. He had loved me and I him, but our placement in time was as wrong as it could have been. I was far too naïve to have been the healing light he needed at that time, and he in that moment had been a broken man. One reduced to feelings of nothingness or loneliness from all of the past emotions he had experienced and lost. I still wished he would have known just how much he meant to me. If he had actually believed that he was good enough for me, if he had known that all I cared about was how happy the presence of my significant other made me, he would have known just how deserving he was of me.

If he had accepted my love, I would never have been brought to feeling as

I do now though. The fairy-tale status of it all takes me back still to this day. I would never have accepted the task of getting his soul back; I would never have discovered what he truly meant to me. I would never have discovered what he would come to mean in the fabrication of my existence. I knew him only in the present state as a man without a soul, not the mate to mine which I had fallen in love with so long ago. I looked forward to, more than anything, the day where our souls, his and mine, would meet again face to face; each embodying its respective half. This was the way that it had to be almost essentially to have been everything that it was. The most poetic and romantic of perfections, I myself could not have imagined a better story. It was almost as though it was by sheer nature, necessity.

Perhaps I am the least qualified to be accurately labelling what is necessity and what is simply a want. On some level, I'd like to think at least, if I had thought it to be necessary then wouldn't its necessity have been just as plausible to me as it being a want might have been to another? I can imagine an instance where the opposite might actually ring true. I might not believe that something one person considers to be a necessity as one, but I may consider it to be simply a want. Like for some, driving an automobile to work every day might be a need, especially if they had quite a distance to commute every morning. However, I cannot find the use of a car to be anything but a want for in my current location, I can reach my work and all other areas of my life by foot. So the concept of necessity then becomes a variable based upon the individual's life. I cannot then say that I am in the wrong for any one of my considerations of necessities, just as others could not say they are in the wrong for theirs. This is as logical as the comparison can get, I must say, for it provides an explanation for each side of the possible outcomes. Therefore, what I consider to be necessary must be, with respect to its relation in my life, just that.

Truthfully, I did not want to feel the way that I did about Vergil. I had been raised my whole life to have existed independently, without feeling as though I needed anyone else. I had gone my whole life without anyone else, without any companionship, and from what I understood, was completely fine with it. It is possible that I was not happy, but my life was liveable nonetheless. It was fine for I did not know what it was like to be happy. To feel as though I might have been a part of something larger than myself. To feel as though I was connected to another being that I had never known before. Someone that I had only shared a small fraction of my life with, yet in that small fraction, would have come to have been impacted by them on a level that would affect the way that I was to live out the rest of my life.

Hindsight is always perfect and this case was no exception to that. I almost thought it possible at one point, for Vergil to have known all along that this was simply the way that it had to be. It was necessary for us never to have been together for any sort of change to have occurred in the way both he and I lived our daily lives. I wondered if he had known it all along, and that was why he wasn't able to love me the way that I deserved to be loved. This however, I think more likely, is to be dismissed simply as my anxieties manifesting themselves, for if this had been his game from the start, I do not believe such a façade could have gone on without my suspicion of it. Vergil had, always been impressed with my mind and its sharpness to pick up even the smallest of details, and I believe these to have been real feelings. He was not simply pretending to have been impressed by it; this I do know for certain. For him to have rejected me in such a manner, I am sure of it, was not intentional. He had not known all along of my placement and significance in his life. In knowing this, I understand my knowledge of our previous existences together to be conceivable only in my mind. Even in knowing that I meant something special to Vergil, I knew also that he, no matter how much I wished, had not the ability to understand what it was. For one must have a soul to understand the matters of it, and he had not one to understand them with. He had understood something to have been present, but not what, how, or why. I was the half of the soul that was still embodied and I had known much more about the situation than he did. It was my knowledge and feelings that had in turn led me to have confused them with love. Not that the feelings were not true love, but rather that they were love based on the fact that they were feelings I had never experienced before. I concluded that it was love based on that fact; however the truth remained that it was love sprouting not from ignorance, but rather of a pre-determined fate that I had not before considered. It was all necessity.

I was glad that I was not given a choice in the matter to be honest. A more prefect creature could not have been created to match my soul, and if it was to be fate, then fate it was to be. My soul had been compelled to get Vergil his soul back, not only for him, my true love, but also for itself, so that it might one day have the chance of resting in eternal peace. I believed that I myself would never have been able to have ever fabricated a better love story than the one that I was living, and it was all thanks to Vergil. Necessity ringing true, presented me with everything that I needed to have made the impossible possible. This was the life that was going to count. I had lived many a life prior to this one, perhaps without the ability to have made a difference about this, perhaps without having gone my entire life unfulfilled having not met him. One thing was for certain, and that was that I had everything I needed in this life to make it the one that would count. The one where even if I did not succeed, I would have done everything possible to facilitate its success in the next. This life, within all its conditions, I believed, was the one that would allow me to finally be free.

Although discouraged, I absolutely cannot bring myself to believe that all hope has been lost in the pursuit of fulfilling my soul's purpose and finally being able to rest in peace. If this was the case, I am sure of it, I would never have been given the opportunity to live this life to begin with. It simply cannot be over, for if that was the case, then the only conclusion one would be able to come to would be that there is no existence of any sort of God, or rather that he does exist only as an entity that does not believe in the idea of everyone deserving to be happy in the end. It cannot simply be my misfortune to live the life that I do.

No, my soul mate lost his soul to the Devil and since I am damned to live my life over and over again as a soul on this earth without ever having the chance of escaping my own Hell, then surely there is not a God to be found in this forsaken place. Everyone must be given the chance, everyone must have the option, no matter how difficult or hard it is to obtain. It must be present. Just as the option must be there for me, the option of Vergil reclaiming his soul must be present. This is the case where they shall go hand in hand and walk each other to the finish. Vergil shall get his soul back, and I shall be set free. They go so perfectly together. I understand it only as having been the by-product of a necessity that had existed once, and one that still surely must.

A Strange Occurrence

I made the mistake of thinking that if I hung out with new friends, if I tried to meet new people, that it would help speed up the amount of time it would take to get over living my life without you. I believed that if I made new friends, went out with people from work, that it would all work out, that this had all just been a part of my life that did not matter. One day I would be working or hanging out and I would meet someone new to fall in love with. I wanted to believe that through making new friends I would broaden my horizons in the city and I would be one step closer to finding true happiness, since it was not mutually felt that I was to find it with you.

I liked to believe that this whole situation was going to pass, that eventually time would have done its duty to me, and I would no longer spend my evenings in solitude. It made sense to me that even if I was still gut wrenchingly upset all the time, going out with friends might make me feel better. If not internally, then only externally for a few hours. Even that short amount of relief from my emotions might prove a fantastic escape; one that would definitely be greatly appreciated.

A few acquaintances that I knew from my place of employment had invited me to go play billiards with them after we had all finished our shifts. Of course I agreed to accompany them; I needed to forget, no matter what I had to do in order to do it. The individuals that had invited me were not to say, the normal group type of people that I would find myself hanging out with, but they were friends nonetheless. I was hesitant about going out that night, just as I was hesitant about leaving my house for anything except going to work or school. It was a step outside of my comfort zone. One that I really did not want to take, but one that I had to. I looked at myself in the mirror as I was getting ready and I asked myself to come to terms with what I saw. A woman whose face wore only sadness, that was starting to show as clearly as the sun shone in the morning sky. It had once been so full of youth, of life, and of happiness. It seemed only to be filled now with haunting memories of a love that once was, of one that no longer existed. I made a feeble attempt at a smile. I was not fooled into believing for even such a minuscule moment, that I was happy. The sorrow most definitely showed through all else. This only confirmed to me that I did in fact need to at least try something to amend my soul. I knew this night would have been nothing in comparison to the fantastic summer; the summer that now only haunted me. It remained only a whisper of my life, but I felt so alive, so real, and so defined in its midst.

I did not know what to wear that evening. It was a simple casual get together, but that did not stop my anxieties from festering in my mind. I have never been in a situation where I have felt as though I was uncomfortably out of place from being overdressed. In this logic I decided to wear a lovely black corset and jeans. The outfit itself was simple enough, yet it accentuated the tantalizing parts of the female body most successfully. When I arrived at the establishment I was surprised to see that I was not the most indecently dressed person there. There were a few different females that were wearing practically no clothing. I never really understood why some women dressed like this for it left little, if no room for the imagination to work over the male mind. This might be a reflection of my personality though, since I have always been one for exercising ones imagination. A reflection of the time however, was the fact that women were wearing less and less clothing. Provocative in a sense, but more so a reflection of the liberation that was taking place for the female race in the passing of time within this century. To dress the way that one felt is an expression of our time, and currently, it was not solely limited to the expression of men.

I dressed in a fashion that made me content also. There really was nothing on this earth like the feeling of a corset snugly fitting ones upper body. Cinching the waist to remarkably small widths, the seductive criss-cross backing holding it all together, and the exhilarating accentuation of the curvatures of ones breasts up until the point that there were almost springing from the boning was a feeling that felt right to me. It was in that moment where you would know that it was on you properly. By the end of the evening I would be most content with my fashion choice, for it was in wearing this corset that made escaping into the night possible. I mention this article of clothing for the importance that I believe it to hold within the larger, broader context of the whole story. The fact that I have always been drawn to corsets, even as a child, makes me think that they serve to prove the point that my soul might have come to be from another time. Within the dream also, the woman that I had grown up to be only a reflection of externally wore corset tops all the time. Perhaps it is a fact that should not bear any importance, but I would simply like for it to be put into the open that the possibility for it to bear significance is present also. I shall leave it up to your discretion to determine whether or not it bears any significance to the story.

As the night progressed, I found myself at the mercy of my fellow, now intoxicated, co-workers. As it usually occurs when the spirits are flowing, things started to escalate into scandal. The sheer angle of my corset top did not help my situation out either. The males of the group were taller than me, and I did not figure this in to my thoughts when I chose my outfit that night. My corset top was now being mistaken as an interest in them, when in all reality it was only for me to feel comfortable in the setting that I was in. I had simply gone that night as a feeble attempt to forget about Vergil, and now all eyes were on me, my corset, and my bosoms as they tantalized everyone in their wake. Luckily, it would also be this top that would help me exit this uncomfortable situation and lead to the safe comfort of my welcoming bed.

Right about at this time, another woman came and started a bit of a stir up within the group. One of my male compatriots had been waiting to use the washroom. The men's washroom had been occupied for, what I could deem as, at least ten minutes. Since it was rather silly and awkward to be standing in front of the washroom facilities, he decided that since the female washroom was vacant, to use it instead. Only a few minutes had passed when the woman showed up. She asked me if my friend was in the bathroom, to which I responded that he in fact was. In hearing that the occupant was male, she immediately began assaulting the door. She banged on it furiously and started shouting for him to get out. He opened the door quite aggressively and left. She said a few words about how upset she was that he had been using the female's washroom when he was a male, and had no business being in there. Being the type of male to not have much respect for females, he disregarded the words she spoke and simply sneered to respond. She slammed the door and proceeded to do whatever business she had set out to do in the washroom. The only problem that remained was that she was not entitled to these facilities next. I had been waiting for him to finish before she had. And I really needed to use the facilities.

I thought it futile, but I attempted to knock on the door anyways. I did not use excessive force or anger; I only knocked in a non-threatening fashion. I'd like to believe that she did not open the door the first few times that I knocked because she had thought that it was my co-worker trying to make her further upset. It was in my thinking this that initially prompted me to knock with ease. I did not want her thinking that I was him. A few minutes had passed, and to be completely honest, it seemed to me that she had now surpassed the time spent in the washroom by my co-worker even. I knocked once more, and finally, she opened the door. Just a crack to peek at who was knocking. When she saw that it was me, she opened the door slightly a bit more, I explained to her that I was actually next in line to use the washroom and that I really had to go. She was fine with that, and since I was not male, opened the door for me to come in and join her.

It was a bit awkward being in a single stall washroom with another person, but she was simply reapplying her makeup and I did really have to vacate my bladder. It was at this moment that she noticed my corset, and told me how sexy it was. I looked up at her, still vacating my bladder, and thanked her for the compliment. I also shared how it was this exact corset that was also the cause for most of my troubles this evening. I told her that I was going through a rather tough time and that I only went out tonight to try and help alleviate some of the mental pain I had been having of late. I explained to her that I was receiving an unwanted level of attention from the group that I was with, and because I was a virgin, was upset with the impression that they were taking away from my attire. I really did not like that everyone thought that I did not have any morals. I personally did not understand exactly how the correlation between a corset top and having no morals or respect for yourself ever even had the option of surfacing, but it did that night.

She looked at me and asked me if I was being serious, she wanted to know if I was in fact a virgin. I looked at her and confirmed once again that I was. She looked at me in the most bewildered fashion and told me some words of wisdom that I believe I will never forget. She looked at me enviously and told me to hang onto my virginity as long as possible, because I didn't know what life was like without sexual relations. This was true. I did not know what it was like to not have that in your life, because it was something I did not miss. It was something that I never had, and therefore, I lacked the ability to miss it.

This lead me to wondering though, what did she mean in saying that? I wondered just how substantial the impact of sexual activity might have on one's life. I wanted to know. To know, however, would also require my knowledge of what it was like to live without sexual activity and I did not know what that was like. I planned on following her advice, for I really did not want to go and find out what life without it was all about. For the time being I thought it wise to stay the way that I was, for it was now common knowledge for every part of myself to know that I would only have given myself to Vergil. Now that this possibility no longer existed, I no longer had the problem of worrying about sexual activity.

I snapped back to reality, to our lovely scene in the washroom. I looked at this woman and thanked her for her insight. She was a woman who, as far as I could see, had experienced the tragedies of life and love. She wore it on her face, just as we all have. After I finished, I emerged from the washroom, with my hair tousled which added to the element of curiosity. Everyone proceeded to ask me what had happened in the bathroom with her. I smiled at them devilishly and told them to use their imaginations if they hoped to figure it out. No harm no foul.

He Festered Within Every Crevice of My Life

I didn't know if I could call him a dirty boy quite exactly, but I knew he had had sex with a slew of different girls and I wanted to lick him clean. That seemed like the only logical route to take. I was really a good girl, so if there was any possibility of his member being given a good thorough cleaning, I was surely the girl for such a task. I don't know why he wouldn't let me attempt such things. I mean seriously, at this point all I could think about was his immense firm penis breaking my dripping wet tight pussy as it has never been done before. I think that made my wantonness for him all the more worse; the fact that I had never had sex before, or any sort of intense relation, like the one that I had with him in my mind now. It was the fact that I knew such fantasies as neither fact or fiction. It was some strange warped middle between the two, occurring only within the confides of my mind, making everyday life all the more difficult to live.

I imagined him showing up completely out of the blue one day on my doorstep. Shortly after he would ring the door bell and begin to knock furiously as I hurried down the stairs bouncing in my step wearing a skimpy little outfit; a low cut black top pulled down to show the lacy bra that was waiting for him underneath, and a short frilly skirt deemed all the more insatiable by the accompanied patterned tights I had on. He would begin pounding on the door at my inabilities to answer it right away at his first will, and when I would open it finally, his arm would be still in the motion of pounding and he would just miss sticking me. He did not want to do such things, he did not want to hurt me.

Realizing that my attire had now suited his initial game, he used his other arm to grab my neck and pin me right up against the mail box, still outside. As I moaned and laughed in seductive pleasure, both of our heads turned. We realized that there had been other spectators watching that were now concerned, that this was no longer a private affair. He let go of me as soon as he realized it too, and grabbed my hand to hold it. As we held hands we entered into my home and walked up the stairs to my bedroom, both gripping onto one another as tightly as humanly possible for the anticipation was eating away at both of us now. With the smirk that I had come to know so well in his presence posted on my face, I twisted the door knob and began to open the door. Before I finished, he let go of my other hand and threw me into the door just in time to walk through it before I hit the wall. I turned around as I fell onto the bed and was now facing him sitting down with my legs crossed, still wearing the smirk only he had ever given me to do so with. As he came to stand closer to me, he put his hand along my leg, and in bending over to reach it, ran his hand up my thigh. Just as this small and sultry action brought me to squeal and accept that I had hopelessly lost this fight of restraint against him, his hand stopped moving up right as it reached the hem of my skirt on my upper thigh. I propped myself back up to sit, no longer wearing his smirk, but rather a look of sheer confusion. The smirk however, as interchangeable as it was and had always been, was being worn on his face now. He brought his other hand up to meet its opposite, and with one swift and calculated movement, ripped a gaping hole in my tights exposing my saturated wet underwear.

How dare he rip my tights so viciously? This was completely unacceptable. I rather quite liked those tights, and that was the last straw. While his hand moved up the naked skin of my upper thigh to reach me, I pushed him forcibly away from me and onto the bed. Last time I wasn't even given the chance to take his clothes of and now, he attempted to do so on me for the second time. Yeah right. As he sat back up in to the bed I pushed him back down and sat on top of his legs, still with my tights completely ripped open. I was closer to him now and I made sure he could still feel how wet I was against his legs. At first I was still hesitant, but I took one of my hands out from behind me and put it on his belt and with the other, I unzipped the fly of his pants. I actually had no idea what to do next. I knew this moment felt right, and I had gone over it a million times in my head, but now I was nervous and my fear of messing it all up was back again. Not this time.

I took his belt out of its loop and pulled it away from his pants. I threw it on the floor and then turned back to him. It seemed for the first moment since our fates began to intertwine, that we were now both wearing this ever so transparent smirk. I unbuttoned the top of his pants to expose the tip of his large, expanding cock. He was so big, I never understood how it never became apparent through the seaming of the clothes he wore before, to even others that he surrounded himself around. Initially, I put my hand on him over his boxers, then it dawned on me that such an action was not the most ideal to execute in that moment, and so I withdrew. As he looked up in confusion from the other side of the bed I looked at him also. As we made eye contact I bowed my head and put it to him and as firmly as I could, I stuck my tongue out and licked from the base of his shaft all the way to the tip and as I finished, let out a fantastic moan of satisfaction. I had been wanting to do that for quite some time now, and now that I have, can say that it was as magical as I had imagined it to have been. I placed my hand on him once more and simply began to rub up and down, back and forth, and side to side. I could tell that he liked it because his eyes were now closed and his mouth was open as his breathing began to deepen.

I didn't want to stop touching him, but I wanted to proceed to another step. So, I pulled his boxers right down to his knees, exposing his sizeable penis in all of its raw glory at last. All I had waited for, all of my longing for him, for this moment, for this love, was in front of me at last. I licked him once more as I had before, from the base of his shaft to the tip, this time using my hand to follow my tongue along the opposite side. I licked my lips a few times to make sure they were as moist and accommodating as they could have possibly been. I opened my mouth as wide as I possibly could and stuck my tongue out to cover the bottom of my teeth as my mouth took in as much of him as it could without gagging. I was surprised to find that most of his shaft fit into my mouth, even as erect as he was now, I still managed to get most of him into my mouth without much difficulty. I didn't know how this was possible but he seemed to taste even better than the last time, and I wished I could have licked his balls while he was still fully in my mouth, but he was too long, or rather my mouth was too small, to do so. I went up and down a few times like this, slowly at first, then getting much faster. Realizing that I had forgotten I had hands to help me in all of this, I added one of my hands in to help stroke the part of his cock that wouldn't fit into my mouth, and used the other to massage and hold his testicles. Every so often, just to add a bit of spice and surprise, I would either choke myself by taking a bit too much of his cock in my mouth, or take him out of my mouth altogether and suck on his balls, and the lower part of his shaft. I had read somewhere, perhaps some magazine, that men liked this.

This went on for quite a few minutes. By no means had I gotten tired or bored of anything that I was doing to please him, but rather I worried that the repetition was boring him. So I attempted to step my game up a notch, and this time when I took him out of my mouth, and as I stroked him up and down, I gathered a nice glob of spit and sloppily kissed it onto his penis. I don't know whether or not he liked that, but as soon as I did it, he looked up at me, and our eyes met once more. This time however, he did not look as pleased as he had been the first time. As I rubbed my spit onto his now freshly lubricated swollen penis, he got up and pushed me down onto the bed to face me. He caught the surprised look that I was wearing on my face from such a sudden change in movement and took advantage of it to deeply kiss me. I loved how passionate a kisser he was. Both times he had been so wanting, yet still gentle.

It seems the roles were reversed now for as he kissed me and used his hands to pull down my bra and caressed my perky nipples in the cold air of the room, I could feel how wet I had made his cock with my mouth as he pressed up against my thigh. With one of his hands he reached around to my back and without effort, successfully unclasped by bra and ripped it off. He took his lips away from mine and as my eyes opened to question why he did so, looked at me and smiled. It was not the smirk that I had come to know and wear so well. It was a smile of accepting warmth and welcome. I don't think I had ever seen him smile so simply and truly ever before in my life. He was beautiful when he smiled like this. It only lasted for a few intense moments before he began to kiss me again, and as he moved his hands down from my breasts to the top lace of my underwear. I couldn't help but let out another excepting whimper of excitement. He grabbed my underwear at the hip and brought his hand around the back to grab my panties, pulling upwards so it made a sort of thong; it was also rather unexpected which kept my moan going on for longer than it probably should have.

After he pulled them up, he brought his hand forward from the start of my bottom all way to the front crease of my pussy and smirked as he felt how wet it was before pulling them right down. I was elated that he didn't decide to rip them off as he did with my tights. I mean matching sultry lingerie was expensive, and I was not one to waste things of great cost so hastily. The tights I didn't mind about for even though I favoured them quite a bit, I had not any sort of personal attachment to them as I had to Vergil and they also only cost a few dollars. Obviously without my help, there was no possible way Vergil could have gotten my panties off, so I helped and pulled them down as he did. In the process of pulling them down my leg, my hand brushed past his juicy dick which reiterated my confidence level in terms of whether or not I had done a good job. I was definitely worried that I hadn't; I wanted to be the very best that I could have been for him.

It was funny to think in that moment how we both the same end goal of being our best, yet it meant two very different things. He was to be his best for me, in terms of being as accommodating yet firm enough in my eyes to have been the perfect combination of rough love for my tender virgin body. I liked his strength, perhaps I even envied it a little. It wasn't that I wanted him to be overbearing and forceful with me, for we both knew that I couldn't handle that sort of behaviour initially, it was that even within my limitations I wanted it to be present because it was what I knew I liked. From my angle, I didn't want to hold the general stereotype that virgins held in this society as not only religious and prude, but rather naïve and unknowing of all the nautities of sex. No, I did not want to be that. Sex was not complicated, and there was no possible way, that even if you were a remotely intelligent female, that you couldn't expose yourself to different subjects surrounding sex so that at least when the time came, you would have had all of the necessary implementations you deemed to be important at your disposal. There really was no reason to be a stiff board during the first time you had sex if you were a virgin. Well at least for me, it just didn't make sense. So in the time that Vergil and I spent apart, I studied, I tried my best to learn the order of operations before attempting to solve the problem. As this ran though my mind, my hand came to pass along his cock, and I realized that I had done my job well. That this was quite likely the most perfect example that anyone could find as being the prefect synergy of reflection between us.

I had no idea how this happened, but once again I found myself completely naked while he still had clothes on. How did this happen a second time? Granted he only had his shirt on, and his pants were pulled almost all the way down, so there was definitely progress that had been made; but still, he shouldn't have had any clothes on at this point. Even though I was ready to accept him, I did not find him suitable of such actions yet because he was still wearing his clothes. It took a lot of effort for me to compose myself because I had become so hot and entangled in his web of lust that I knew little about how to conduct myself now. Nonetheless, I propped myself up on the bed and grabbed his shirt to pull it off. Initially he looked at me with a bit of concern. Perhaps because he though I was going to rip it off, but the look of reject and confidence for it on my face quickly dissolved that. It was not as smooth as all of the undressing he did on me, but I managed to pull his tunic off with a level of ease I could label as success. His pants weren't really on, so once this was done, I quickly hoped off the bed and pulled them off onto the floor. We were finally both completely naked, and it was fantastic.

I wanted to get back on the bed with my face placed down against it and place my legs just off the side in the air so Vergil would have the best possible angle to see just how wet and ready I was to accept him. It was a very primitive and raw position to be in, and as much has I had wanted to get into it, I didn't because it just didn't seem like a good position to be in having sex the first time. For me, this signalled to turn myself down a bit. I was getting flustered and ahead of myself. Vergil took this time to pull a gold foil wrapped condom out of the back pocket of his pants.

Actions have reactions, and I was glad to have one to this action. I ran up to the coffee table and picked up the half-used pack of birth control that I had started taking as sheepishly as I can admit, exactly for this reason. I might have hastily thrown it at him in an unexpected fashion, but it didn't matter because he caught it in his hands and smiled at me while he threw both it and the condom against the wall with a twisted look of both satisfaction and surprise on his face. As surreal as it was to me also, I finally had an upper hand on him. He wasn't expecting this level of careful anticipation and calculation from me, but why not? Who wants to have sex for the first time through a condom. No, I wanted to feel him inside of me, especially since it was him, and well, his dick was deserving of such.

He pulled me back on the bed finally and gave me a gripping hug that lasted for more than a few seconds. I don't know what he felt in hugging me for such a lengthy time, but I know I felt his heart beat against mine after the first few seconds and it was amazing to note that they were also in sync with each other. This moment really could not have been any level more of perfect than what it was now. We hadn't even had sex yet and I was ready to come all over him. All of the factors I was considering in my mind now, they all added up to such an intense feeling. As my mind wandered, Vergil brought his hands across my breasts, and made his way down to my pussy rubbing the outside a few times to spread the concentrated wetness around before inserting one of his fingers into me. I was too wet to only accept one of his fingers, too enthralled to do so. I needed more, I needed as much of any part he wanted to offer me inside me as fast as he could possibly do it.

I grabbed onto his hand and put another finger in for him. I figured why not, so I let go of the sheets that I was gripping onto for dear life and grabbed his penis, which to my disappointment, was not as slippery as it had been a few minutes ago, but was still just as large. Well something had to be done about that, he needed to be just as wet as I was. He found a spot inside me with his fingers that I didn't even know existed, and as he stroked inside, it felt so good, so warming. It was definitely distracting because I lost all my abilities to think or execute any actions. Nonetheless, I took control and gathered myself to take his hand out of me. What a mess I had made all over him; my juices were all over his fingers so I placed them in my mouth and cleaned them off. Seriously, the look on his face was one that I could never come to apply a price to. But in reality, who was I to not see how I tasted? I had done this a few times before touching myself thinking about him and I came to the conclusion that I did actually taste good, not sour or anything terrible, not sweet like a fruit either, but rather like a candied bacon. Sweet but also with tones of meat infused into the palette. I sucked his fingers clean and dry like they were his cock.

He put his hand on my neck and pressed me into the bed ever so gently, and as he began to lick my nipples, made his way down my torso to my pelvic region. I wasn't ready for him to do that to me. I propped myself up a little bit and shook my head in disagreement, it just wasn't my thing. I didn't really want him seeing what I tasted like, or at least I wasn't at that point yet in with the level of trust that I had for him. He might have been used to girls tasting better, like candy or fruit. I wasn't certain that he would have found me as appealing after if he had put his lips on my pussy.

So I let out a smile because I knew that it was time for him to finally break my seal and put his throbbing cock inside of my over prepared cunt. I put my hand on his cock and with a few last affirming strokes of his member I lifted my legs up and placed them on his shoulders since I was flexible enough to do so. There was a moment of hesitation, were he just held his cock over me and rubbed it back and forth. It definitely might have been to get him as wet as he could possibly have been if he wanted to avoid really hurting me as he went in, but I think the anticipation of him doing so as he rubbed the outside hurt more. I felt him place his penis in between the two pieces of skin around my vagina; he was about to enter. He looked me in the eyes and gave me a kiss on the cheek. As the latter occurred, he slowly moved forward into me.

He let out a moan as I did now also, it was so tight down there. I could feel every part of him inside me; in my tight little pussy. I winced a bit, because to be completely honest it did hurt quite significantly when he trusted into me, even though it was still very gentile. My emotions lacked any sort of control now. As he proceeded to thrust faster and faster, I couldn't help but feel as though I had begun to constrict, that my pussy was tensing up. How was this possible? I was hoping that the exact opposite would have happened, that his voluptuous dick ought have been able to loosen me up so we could enjoy each other in different positions, not just this silly ancient missionary style. I couldn't let go of my grip on him, this all felt so new, so tight, and so warming. He was going in and out now with much more ease, almost all the way, but this didn't stop me from feeling as though I was tightening up even more. As I closed my eyes with the inability to seize all of the lustful sounds I was making now, I felt a warming sensation, it became stronger as my pussy began to wrap around his cock. I let go and accepted this feeling of love, of warmth, and of intensity. I ran towards it with him now.

And as I opened my eyes reality came to slap me in the face. It was all just a dream, just a fantasy that made me cry in its reality. I woke up and sighed. I knew it could never have been real, I knew that. Perhaps my love for Vergil may not ever come to be known in time as real, as something that can be concretely defined. This fantasy, this longing for him, has only progressed with the passing of time. Even you can so plainly see, the distance between us has slowly festered in my mind and encompassed all aspects of my life. There was no part of me that didn't feel as though I was an extension of him; and if the present theories on dreams mean anything, then my inner psyche too was clearly still very affected by this fantastical man.

A Harder Lesson to Learn

Last winter it was very cold in the city, and of course the present winter season followed in this trend. Since there was ice everywhere, one had only to skate along thin sheets of it until they reached the side walk, which even then, was always filled with a very wintery snow slosh. Often times, such factors rendered it much more difficult to travel by foot anywhere, even if it was just to the bus stop.

When spring finally came around and I finally decided to leave the house wearing a pair of shorts to meet with a friend I had been in correspondences with throughout the winter months, I had not seen her for what seemed to me as being at least a few months. It was very possible that the time period in which I did not see her was actually longer than that. Lately, time has simply been slipping through the cracks of my fingers similarly to the essences of life it shares with the ever so volatile water. Although my palm was tightly clasped, my fingers felt as though they were glued together in concentration to accept the moments of time showering into them. However this was not the case, for I am finding lately that no matter how hard I try, no matter how hard I clasp my fingers together I cannot escape this melting of time that has begun to occur. It was the result of this occurring that kept me somewhat from seeing any one of my friends for quite a long while.

When I arrived at her house, it seemed almost as though there had not really had been a significant time lapse that had passed since the last time we had seen each other. I have always believed that if you ever have a friend with whom you did not see for a long while, but still had the ability to greet one another as though the time you had spent apart was not significant at all, then that was the very definition of a true friendship. A level of understanding that no one else could have understood between the two of you, which perhaps the two themselves, would not even come to openly understand might be present. To pick up the conversational tones of a friendship that had experienced a time lapse is a sure-fire way to know whether or not that person is a true friend.

However, almost instantly after we began conversing she noticed that my legs were covered in a large amount of severe bruises. Mostly, they concentrated specifically around my knees, because I had fallen quite a bit on the ice that winter, but I was in no position to let something as unimportant to me as bruises on my body interfere with my enjoyment of the finally changing weather. She asked me what had happened and if I was okay because the bruises looked to be quite aggressive in nature. She asked me how many times I had fallen that winter. As a response I simply looked at her for a moment, squinting a bit more crucially then I should have, only because she inquired instantly about how many times I had fallen. It was the first time I became extremely puzzled because I had never considered the perspective that was involved with such an action as falling before. I hesitated for a moment and then responded that I had gotten up eight times.

The reaction on her face was one of confusion also. When she inquired further about my response, I explained to her that I found it more relevant to tell her the number of times that I had gotten up as opposed to the number of times that I had fallen. I wonder why the significance was always put on the fall, never anything ever mentioned about when a person got up. The number of times you fall only becomes significant when it is the same amount as the number of times you got up, because ultimately that would mean that the last time you fell, you did not get up.

It is only in mentioning this that has brought me to think of another scenario in my mind, which occurred to me previously, but was now relevant to the story. Rather sickeningly, I was at an event where I had been walking down a flight of marbles stairs when my shoes, which caused a bit of difficulty to walk in because they were plainly a booted heel one size too big, caused me to lose my place of step. Like I normally do, I fell in the most intense fashion. I went down from the second step to the very last one. When I realized that my foot had slipped and that I was going to fall, I let go of the railing that I was holding onto because I knew that it would have been too difficult to hang on. It seemed probable to me, that in the moment, it would have caused my body more damage to have tried to hold on, of course with the option of possibly failing to do so being the reason why it might have made my situation worse.

I immediately understood that I as falling down the flight of stairs, and as I rolled right down to the bottom, with every bump that occurred in segments from the breaks in the stairs, lovely bruises that matched the zig-zagging pattern of the stairs appeared along the length of my body. I had about ten different bruises from the tip of my toes to the top of my head. I'd like to think that I fell with grace, at least onto the ground that I got up from after, thankfully because I had the ability to brush myself off and continue walking. I was thankful also that only one other person had been looking at me to the point where they would have been able to identify me out of a crowd at a later date. It has never been my preference to be known as the madam that fell down a flight of stairs simply because she lost her step, as she usually does. However, I will be forever known to the gentleman who witnessed my fall and getting up as the girl who rolled down a flight of marble stairs and managed to successfully get up without having been seriously damaged. I was glad that this first impression was made just as fast as it had ended. I have never met that person again, nor do I ever wish to.

When this incident happened however, and shortly after, I did not really feel as though I was in any amount of pain that was too unbearable to handle. It did not, at least to me, seem to be that bad. This is a reflection of me in the sense that pain has never really been something that I have been able to measure with much accuracy. It's not that I don't feel pain, which does occur sometimes, but rather I feel as though my mind has somewhat over the course of this life certainly, perhaps others also, been programmed to not acknowledge pain as well as other do. When I woke up the next day though, I can safely say that my body had registered the pain quite successfully. It was painful to even move. Every bruise on my body had left quite a significant mark, and it seemed that I was unable to move without affecting at least one of the bruises. The worst one was thankfully, on my leg, where it did not come into contact with a lot a weight. However, all of the bruises were now black and ranging from the size of a tennis ball, to the one on my leg which was the size of a plate.

I find it very difficult to relay the fact that it was not only the physical pain that was a by-product of my falling that disturbed me. It was the feelings of sadness and sombre tones of sorrow that accompanied my physical feelings about the bruises the day after. To simply look at them made me think of you, Vergil. The week of physical recovery that occurred after that night was only supplemented by a week of mental awareness and torment as to how much the bruises on my body reminded me of you, which made me cry more times than I'd like to admit. Even when I was only walking, it was a very painful task. This pain only reminded me of you, because you were the only other person to have inflicted a level of pain on me that was as high as I was feeling right now. I realized that I enjoyed that one faithful night so much because for the first time, you made it possible for me to blame someone else for all of the marks on my body as opposed to the usual explanation; that I was just insanely clumsy. It made me upset, that for the first time in my life I had you within my reach, I had the ability to place the blame on somebody else that was not myself. Every single other time in my life, I was the only person that I had to blame when any sort of accident occurred.

I have fallen so many times. I am a very skilled and experienced faller, which at least to me, meant that I was also very experienced in the art of getting up. To be honest, it is quite possible that in all actuality for me to consider falling only as getting up might be the only option that I have available for my thoughts to unfold in order for my brain to consider it as anything else might cause severe mental damage to one's mind. Consider if you were simply a clumsy individual. If you had been clumsy your whole life, one might then warp their mind to thinking that there was something wrong within themselves because they fell way more than others and were always bruised up. Feeling like this might have been the result of self-discovery, meaning that you developed this as a feeling over time in simply noticing these things for yourself, or other catalysts may have introduced these feelings to you, via a bully or a parent, and of course, these feelings would have resonated overtime also. By nature or nurture then, feelings of clumsiness could resonate as feelings of insecurity and of not being good enough because you were always the clumsy one. The feelings of insecurity that would accompany this clumsiness would then resonate and the clumsiness would also then be caused by the feelings of insecurity. It would essentially be one big and vicious circle that would continue, most likely, for the rest of person's life just as it is currently doing so in my life.

But the moral of the story here was that I missed you more than I have ever missed anyone in my life that week. I was all bruised and banged up, and all I could think about was how much I missed the one person who relieved me of all my feelings of insecurity and clumsiness. In a way, it was the bruises on my body that reminded me once that I had found someone that made me feel for the first time, like it wasn't my own fault for being banged up. Presently, they reminded me only of the fact that the reality where I felt good about myself being covered in bruises that I didn't inflict on myself was one of the past. Now, I had only the pain and memories of a past that will never come to be my reality to cry myself to sleep with. The constant pain that I felt both mentally and now physically, reminded me again that I was the only factor that served to explain who was to blame for the pain I was feeling. I wasn't good enough. I would never be good enough. You are perfect, and I remain only a broken girl with no hopes or dreams that didn't end in a happiness that was an extension of you.

The Concept of Love

I tried to understand the concept of love. I find essentially, that this was something that was of the utmost difficulty for me only due to the fact that it was one of the only concepts that I had not ever been familiarized with before. Having said this, it made me uneasy to think about this whole ordeal, around everything that had to do with Vergil because I cannot say indefinitely that I am certain that it was love. Not to say that it might have been love mixed with additional factors as well, but I had never been in love before, so I know not if it was for certain. It was a new feeling, a new set of experiences, a new concept. It makes sense to me to think of this fact as the reason proving that it was in fact love. For if it was a feeling that I had known before of some other affection, then surely I would have been able to recognize it as just that. I believe my ignorance around it all is proof that I was in fact in love with Vergil because I had not known if I loved him or not. There was never an incident in my life where, for example, I did not know whether I was angry or not. Whether I was happy or not. These emotions and feelings, along with all the others that I have ever experienced in my life are ones that were always clearly defined. The ambiguity of love is one that I am not sure I will ever have a clear definition for. It pains me to say this, but I fear more than anything that I might never love another the same way that I did Vergil.

Sure, as time goes on I might find another, to settle down and enjoy each other's company in order to facilitate the simple inner workings of a human's life and needs. But simply put, It fears me greatly that I have now known to understand exactly what the concept of love was, and now that I have done such, I will never have the opportunity to become as confused about it as I was in my time spent with Vergil. It is something of great interest for me, the ambiguity of love. As I come to understand, it holds in its hand the most important element; that is the element of surprise. You never know when it is going to find you, when it shall strike, you know not of its unruly lack of control or its strangeness of heart. The moments that build up to its realization, come about only of course, after the feelings themselves have built up internally to the point where they are the only thing you think about.

That is the strangeness of love. It comes about only it its entirety. To miss one, or rather to feel as though you enjoy the company of a person is simply not what love is. I believe that the definition of love should include the kind of feelings that they install in a person. Love is when you long to spend every moments with someone, when you cannot wait after a long day to see them, when no matter what sort of situation, you cannot for any reason, be mad or upset with them. That is love. It is a thing that does not abide to time, for it is timeless.

The dictionary has given me the definition of love as being an intense feeling of deep affection. If this sort of definition adds to anything, it adds to the ambiguity that surrounds love. Around the different types of love, and around the other emotions that accompany love. I suppose that the purpose of a dictionary is to give the most universally understandable definition of a word to facilitate everyone's understanding of it. For me at least, it is the fact that I have come to know love as a concept much more different and complicated than deep affection. It is the master of all other emotions who bow down to its presence and obey its every rule and demand. This is the power that love holds, it goes above all else. It is the most fantastic of all things. I wonder often if love is solely a human invention, if other living things experience love as we do. I'd like to think of love sometimes, as the thing that separates us as a species from anything else in the universe. We have the ability to love. We have the ability to do anything in love.

I know for certain that one of the factors that lead to the feelings I had for Vergil was my own disposition about myself. I had no love for myself, and wanted only to love another for it was something that I had never done before. That, if anything, was the fault that made my anxiety worse than it had ever been. To feel in love with someone, I would say, ought to be one of the most fantastic feelings in the world. This love was not one that ensued these types of feelings. Not because it was not a true love, but because it was one that occurred whilst my mind was in a state of emotional distress.

I did not care much for myself and in turn had cared more for Vergil than for the wellbeing even of my own self. Call this sadness, depression, or what you will, but I understand these feelings only as having been ones that made the feelings I had for Vergil even more powerful and all the more real. It is the instrument that was my salvation and my damnation. From the beginning I believe it was my inability to love myself that hindered any possible chance at a successful relationship with Vergil. It was also a factor that helped me solidify the feelings I had for him when I began the journey of loving myself and acquiring the feeling of deserving to live. I do now thank Vergil for this, even though I have love and many other emotions for him, I know for certain that the emotions I feel now about myself would not have been possible if our paths had never crossed. It is using this reason that my love for him has become completely solidified. Knowing him helped me love myself. That is certainly the one of the greatest gifts to give someone that I can think of.

There was a certain level of fear that came along with my love for Vergil also. It was very strange, but nonetheless present. It was not the fear of rejection, or of him not loving me, but rather the fear that I myself did not know what love in fact was. I could say that I loved him, but did I really know what love was enough to use the term accurately? That was my fear. I did not know whether or not I actually had fallen for him. I was confused and sad a lot of the time because I had doubts about the love that I had for this man. What a silly thing to think. Of course I loved this man. There was nothing to be afraid of, but that did not keep my mind from instilling it anyways. I had fallen and finally, I did not want to get up.

It was not the fear of being in love that made me ever so weary as time passed. It was all of the other emotions and feelings that came along with its spectrum. It was the embodiment of every emotion. It was complete. I did not understand how or why, but the feelings that came to me when I thought about Vergil were always just this. They were both happy and sad, both joyous and painful. I believe that it was this blending of outputted emotion that led me to understanding my feelings as love. It was this duality of it all, the fact that I loved this man even when he had done something to make me upset. I have been the happiest that I have ever been in my life when next to the presence of this man. I have also been in the darkest corner of my mind in the presence of this man, and so I understood love as being the only option here.

One night, I had been at home preparing myself for bed when my telephone started to ring all of a sudden. I answered, as one should, for I really did not think of who might have been on the other line as negative in anyway. I wasn't avoiding anyone, so I picked it up. It was Vergil. I remember in this moment, in hearing his voice; my heart simply jumped. I was so thrilled to think that he had been thinking of me that night. I was in his thoughts. Me. The girl that had no concept of self-worth or positive things to say about herself had been in the thoughts of the godliest example of a man ever to have been created.

For a moment I was speechless in responding to his greeting. I then answered and agreed to meet up with him that night as we usually did. Usually we corresponded by message or online, never really on the telephone. I believed this time, was the first time he had ever contacted me via an actual phone call. It is so strange to try and understand that even his voice sounded godly. How could one man have possibly embodied so many characteristics of what I would believe to be a God? The answer to that question still seems to run around in my mind without answer. He was quite perfect. I'd like to believe that one day soon, I will have achieved that same level of perfection also. For, if it is possible for one to achieve perfection, I cannot think of any reason why one shouldn't.

Another instance proves the latter of the two examples. It was my birthday and I wanted to celebrate. I had been hoping simply to have a good birthday perhaps with a few spirits, good food, and of course lots of laughter. However, this never occurred, and my birthday came and went. Vergil had forgotten my birthday and I had forgotten that he had. I remembered in that moment I was so angry and enraged, for not a few months earlier I made sure to make his birthday as enjoyable as possible. I didn't even get any effort on his part. It made me so upset. It was a birthday of rather some significance too, and I really wanted to have a good time. He had forgotten completely. Why had he forgot? It was explained to me at a later date by him as having been the by-product of habit, not to be taken personally because he had never remembered the birthdays of anyone. It was simply how he was. I wanted to believe this, and I am pretty sure that there was a point in my life where I did actually. However, as it stands currently, I think back on that day, to my birthday and remember only how poor I felt even weeks after knowing that I had not meant enough to him to have remembered it. It really didn't matter, I had forgiven him. If anything I suppose it was to serve as a lesson of exactly how one might be upset at someone for something, yet at the same time be madly in love with that same person. Forgiveness was easy then.

It was certainly a love that was one sided. I loved him and in return did not really receive much. Such relationships, have and will always be labelled as toxic. When the level of power is not equal, the one that gives more is the one that always end up with less. As painful as it was to admit, that was exactly what was going on with Vergil. I don't think a day would ever come where he would feel as attracted to me as I felt to him in the past. However, there was no chance in Hell that I would not do everything in my power to have the exact opposite result. In turn, it was this lack of love on his part that helped me realize that in the process of falling in love with him, I had never come to love myself. That was the fault that lay in it all. My fatal mistake. I did not love myself. Others love those who love themselves. I realized this too late. It was only once Vergil and I had seized to know each other that I realized that I had not loved myself. I began the most wonderful journey of self-discovery and learned to appreciate myself for who I was. If anyone deserved to love oneself it was I. I was truly unique. I was a fantastically special, and eccentric being.

Not a day will go by where I will not openly admit that I might not ever have come to love myself without having known Vergil, and that it was only the lack of love that he presented to me which allowed me to see truly how much love I had not been receiving, not just from him. One cannot function without love. I have changed the way I live my life because of him. I am learning slowly but surely to believe in the power that is myself. To believe that I am not wrong to love myself above all, because at the end of the day I have only but myself and my word. To close, in a way it was through loving him that I learned to ultimately love myself. I'd like to thank you Vergil for if anything, showing me that it is okay to love oneself, for before I met you, I knew that I did not. Now, I can think not of a more splendid evening than spending some time with myself and my thoughts walking down the cool forest pathways leading to the busy city roads, or sitting in a small isolated coffee shop enjoying a cup. My company, is the best company. And I was glad to have it.

Belief

When I think about him I feel invincible, as though nothing that I have set out to do has ever been impossible, as though I can take on the world. Truly, honestly, and sincerely, I can say that I have yet to discover any evidence proving that anything else except this can be deemed as true. Obviously there are still things in this world that I normally would not able to do for a variety of reasons more than those that serve to explain how they came to surface as truths. However, everything that I have set out to do as a result of thinking about how he made me feel, I have come to accomplish or complete at a rate that I can deem to be the definition of success. It is an absolutely great feeling to have to be completely frank. Feeling as though anything that you have set out to do has come to correlate with the time spent thinking about him is a surreal thing to also be validly able to say is true. It is nonetheless something that I have come to learn to be true. If you could, why would you ever feel as though you would not want to do such a thing? Feeling on a daily basis as though you can accomplish anything that you set out to do is exactly how I want to feel.

Its almost as though I can compare him to some sort of being far beyond me that has the capability of fulfilling my every desire in this current life if I truly remain dedicated to him. If I live my life constantly thinking about him, and living through him, then it seems almost that my life has no negativities, and even if it did embody negativities, they would remain trivial for they would come to be conquered by my belief in him shortly after they surfaced. He has in a way, become a religion to me, or at least I think of his presence in my life now as something that I would consider as being within the definitions of what a religion is. The only aspect that I could not label as an accurate description of a him being my religion is the fact that whenever I do think about him, or attempt something in his name that I would otherwise have deemed to have been impossible, it is within my reach. Not to say that he makes me invincible, but rather the feelings that he has ensued in me are ones that have led me to attempt a quality of life that I never thought I could lead. I knew feeling this way was wrong, it was wrong in general to feel this way about another human being, for they were not a God, they were not a religion.

Many times I had tried to convince myself to stop living my life through him, always to no avail. One day I woke up and while I was getting ready for the day it suddenly dawned on me; it didn't matter whether I lived my life this way or not even if it was wrong. Why wouldn't one live their life in such a positive and fulfilling manner if they could? It mattered not that the inspiration to do so was derived from another human being. Everyday I live inspired, care-free, and dedicated because I met a man once who has allowed me to now live my life in such a fashion. Day after day success finds me when I live through him, as an extension of him. It is only a hard feeling to have given the current circumstances of the situation, but I know how I feel and how he makes me feel. I truly do feel as though at this point in my life, in living it as an extension of him, I have yet to have any feelings of disappointment in myself. Even living in a time where he has no longer given me the option of speaking to him, I do not find any sense of disappointment within either mine or his actions.

All good things do eventually come to an end. Great things also, like their good counterparts find an ultimate demise despite their ability to be quite elongated within the lines of time. Perhaps the feelings that I have for Vergil will come to pass one day, but I know not for certain. Like I have said, these feelings, my love for him, have come to define me as a human being, quite positively and fantastically so. Therefore I can only hope that time will be so kind as to allow me to hang onto these feelings as long as I possibly can. It is rather refreshing to wake up every day thinking that anything you set your mind to, as long as it is within the emotions that Vergil has ensued in me, then all that I attempted would be possible. I have never felt this way about another living thing on this earth ever before, and I do not believe that I will ever again. I say this because now that I know that I do feel like this, that he is the one who made my feeling so positive and successful in my everyday life possible, that I might not ever give up the feelings that I have for him. I tried to logically asses such a statement and all I could conclude was that I knew how I was feeling right now, I knew that I could do anything through him, and I did not foresee forgetting such applicable over in the near future, if ever. Why would I ever want to? I could not think of any reason.

It is nonetheless a hard feeling to have for more than one reason. The first reason is the sheer fact that like most other religions, my beliefs and feelings of euphoria that I have acquired from living my life through him are ones that he will never come to now about. Well, not in this life at least; even though this may be the one that mattered more than any of the others. I can only describe knowing such a fact as one of the most terrible feelings I have ever had, if not the most terrible. If he knew the way I felt about him, and how thinking about him embodied my daily life to an extent one might consider as a deep mental illness, I want to believe that it might have made a difference; that he might have chosen to have given me a chance at being the best thing to have ever happened to him. It remains a hard feeling to have about one person when they cut off communication with you long before you even had the chance to come to terms and conclude exactly how you felt about them. I wish I had the opportunity to tell him truly what he meant to me, and what he still continues to mean to me today.

The second reason is that it puts a concerning level of faith and godliness into another human being. This makes it a hard feeling to have simply because the matters of God's and Devil's are ones that humans have never fully understood due to their nature of being matters beyond our comprehension. Now, I comprehended such notions within a figure living on this earth, and my comprehension of him as a God or a religion has only lead me to make one other conclusion. I know Vergil has not a soul. And so, I'd like to propose the following characteristic of what a God or a Devil might hold.

The two, perhaps brothers, perhaps only acquaintances, perhaps even two separated half's of the same soul, knew that they were the exact opposite of one another. One being holy, representing all of the greatest virtues possible in all their piety. The other, representing all that is to be considered as sinful, wretched, and wrong. The two however, knew not who was to be considered as the first, and who was to be considered as the latter since they had not the souls to do so, they lacked the capability to determine who was good and who was evil. And so, being all mighty beings, creators of the earth, they did just that and created humans to have the capabilities of the soul, a concept that they did not know about for certain, but since they knew each other as exact opposites, knew that a soul would have to embody both of these aspects to understand them fully, in order to deem which one was the good one and which was the bad.

The soul as one complete entity was then, entirely a human creation. I assume this only in knowing that Vergil had not his half of soul to complete mine. I, like the two, have come to know myself as either good or bad, but not definitively one or the other. I know not whether I am the good half or the bad one. Would Vergil have killed himself and damned his soul to rest with the Devil in Hell if he was the half that was good? I wanted to answer this question as obviously as it seemed to have appeared to be answered. But how could a man considered as evil, a man who was living without his soul, have been such a positive impact not only in my everyday life but within my soul also?

Not only did I believe in Vergil as I lived my every day life now without any contact from him, but I believed also in myself; I believed if anything, if in the very least, I had the ability to get him his soul back. I cannot say that I have been given much in this life, certainly you can agree, but I must have the ability to complete my soul, to get Vergil his half back. It seems such a strange thing to believe, even more so surreal now that I don't care that I know such facts as true. I can get Vergil his soul back, life cannot be so cruel as to not even have granted me this ability. Such a feeling, such a belief, is one that is so fuelling and strengthening to the composition of one's life. You can see now exactly why it took me so long to come to terms with how powerful and unstoppable my belief in Vergil made me. It was through this belief in him also, that I came to believe in myself for together, we are one entity.

If we were to have been known then, as one single entity, as two halves of one soul, then it would seem logical for one to be evil and one to be good. It wasn't that I doubted myself as the good half of the soul, it was that Vergil had not his soul to make such a comparison and conclusion to mine with. If he had, this task might have been executed with much more speed, facility, and accuracy. Just because he didn't have his soul, he should not be labelled right away as the evil half. He could very well have been the good half of the soul, and I the evil one. I wished not to think in terms that were so frightening to my inner self, but I mean I could very well be the evil part of the soul. I only thought this through proposing that Vergil might have been the better half of the soul for what he did for me, or at least in his eyes what he did.

There was no way for him to have been evil. He was perfect, he was a God. In living through him I felt a little more like a God each day also. Vergil was not like the Devil because he did not have a soul, but he was not like God either for he was a man. This is why I am so vexed and confused about the emotions that I have regarding him. I have never understood any human to have been as perfect as he, yet he had not a soul. How could the two possibly be true? I hope to say that one day I have successfully figured out such a riddle, for certainly there is an exception to be found within him. Indeed what I knew to be true about him, was true. I was the living proof of that.

Lets face it, I didn't know about what it was like to know someone intimately, and even after all of this has happened and you remain simply a sparkle of my past, I am still unsure of whether or not I know what it was like to have been with you, and to have been everything you wanted in a person. This may have been only because I really misjudged the amount of change that would have occurred in this life; now that you lead it without a soul. You have not the ability to recognize me, or know who I am or what you mean to me, nor are you able to feel. This life was always meant to be hard for one of us. It would have been me if you had lived the rest of your life out and lived on instead of jumping in front of that train.

The Soul of the City

The wonders that this world holds are ones the I cannot come to describe with words accurately, at least within the confides of language which it also offers. I have gone to the farthest end of the Earth that I was able to reach using my meagre earnings I had from saving in between semesters of school, only to find that wherever I go, what ever location I find myself in, and whatever time of day it is, I bring you with me. I travelled to these places, to go somewhere I've never been before, and to see things that matched the same description. The cities that I have travelled to have all been known to have a heart, a personality, or a soul. I know to conclude for certain that a city has a soul is an invalid concept, however I will agree that there is a sort of tone, a sort of presence that a city holds. It may be even described as the presence the city has whether there is people inhabiting it or not; the influence a city could instil in a person is one that is still present even if there was no one present in the city to label it as so. This is the heart of the city, this is what it has to offer us. A constant tone, whether there be people present to accept it or not. The emotions that any given city ensues in the those that find themselves calling such a place home, is definitely something that can be tangibly measured, well within the human faculty of arts that it has influenced. If anything the things that have been created through the emotions of a should be labelled as more tangible a proof than any other scientific reasoning for they hare the things that humans have created though it. It is nothing without us, and us nothing without it. Not to say that we do not have anything without it, but rather the inspiration that it has given us, to do something or to create something, would not exist in our minds if it was not a present concept. The concept itself also, this creativity, these connotations, they would not be transferable to us from the city if we did not inhabit them.

In my travels, I have come to question and understand two rather peculiar yet completely relatable subject concerning the heart of the city and the emotions that it instils in the people that inhabit it. The first being the fact that no matter where I have travelled, the emotions the city has come to inspire me with are ones that have always been attached to Vergil. Why was this? There might have been two different ways to look at why this was. The first, which I think is also the one least likely to be the truth, was the possibility that enough time had not elapsed for me to have left him in the past yet. Whether I wanted to or not, was another question I didn't want to find an answer to. I knew certainly that I did not want to forget about him, because this man, Vergil, has come to influence me more than anything else has ever before. In all of the negative and positive ways possible.

As I have said before I have brought him with me, my fantasies and anxieties around him alike, and he has always been the volatile subject which these cities have influenced me in regards to. It scares me to consider that I might have never received this immense influx of emotion had I not ever met this man. What then could the heart of the city have offered me, if it was not something so true and emotional as being something influenced by Vergil; by the one whom I have come to know as my soul mate? I knew these cities and their embodied hearts had so much to offer me only because I knew him, because I had this story, because love was something the city knew all too well.

The other way to have looked at this was that there was some measurable relationship between the city, its inspiration, and the love that I had for Vergil. What might it have been then? What could the heart of the city and Vergil have possibly had in common? I knew that they both existed as entities that could not quite be tangibly measured, but as things that could only have been measured internally within the person asking such questions. In this case, the person asking the question was me, so perhaps the correlation between the two that I pondered about was only present also because I was the one that was pondering about them. This relationship then, would be only one that existed in my mind; one that was a reflection of the person imagining it. As accurate as this may have been, it did not explain the relationship in its entirety. To do so, the fact that these cities have inspired countless others must also be taken into consideration to provide a more universally applicable conclusion about it. All of these factors, all of these examples, all of these catalysts; they all had to have one thing in common that linked them together.

My search to answer this question came about only after I had travelled to a handful of different cities said to have an inspiring tone to them, and after I realized also, that I had brought Vergil with me to all of these places. Mainly because the city came to inspire me through him. This phenomenon then, could have been understood through three different divisions, the first being myself as the receiver of inspiration, the city providing me with the influx of inspiration, and Vergil being the subject or relevance of the inspiration in my life. When I thought about the origins of such an influx within my mind in these terms, it made its explanation much easier to find. Since two of the variables of myself and Vergil were interchangeable in the sense that they could be preplaced my other entities and defined through their eyes, the only constant variable that remained present was that of the city's inspiration. The constant variable was also the one that was not supported thorough an embodied living human spirit. Yet, this constant variable meant nothing without the two interchangeable ones of human spirit in each of its end. We give it meaning and it gives us the same in return. The city had only inspiration to offer me through Vergil because he was the only living thing that could have been associated with the city through me. I took this conclusion as great news, since I wished to use the inspiration he gave me the best I could, for it was the only one that I have ever received deemed worth doing so to.

Largely then, this inspiration was the by-product of my mind and what it deemed to have been acceptable of receiving such inspiration. But then was it truly only an internally psychological phenomenon? There must have been a reason why Vergil was the subject I deemed to have been deserving of such inspiration. I knew this reasoning as being the fact that I believed him to be someone that I had met before in another life; a life where through the untimely death of my embodied soul in that period, his soul was lost through taking his own life. If this truly was the case, then it made complete sense to me how it was so easy for me to have brought him to all of these cities throughout my travels, and for him to have inspired me through them. This could very well have been exactly why. I was not to have been able to forget him so easily, so carelessly. Getting him his soul back, mending all the past events that have shaped me today to do so, and believing truly through him that this was all possible was the only thing that knew I had to unconditionally do. The city knew this also.

Ghosts

As a child I was, as I am sure many other children were, scared of ghosts. In saying ghosts, I mean to reference the supernatural beings that come about after death. A ghost is the manifestation of the dead, only in being presented to the living. To another of its kind, a ghost might not be identified as such. In children, this fears surfaces merely from not knowing what is true and what is false about ghosts. Sometimes it is the result of not knowing anything, but rather, simply following their friends in believing and agreeing with them when they tell stories about ghosts. Children do not really understand the concept of ghosts. Not to say that they don't understand what they are, but to say that the way in which they legitimize their understanding is much different from that of the same subject as an adult. Children have a sort of lack of knowledge, a certain naiveté included in everything they understand. This is not limited to the understanding of ghosts, but it is included.

For example, my fear of ghosts was quite serious when I was smaller. Most of my prayers, if any, centered on hoping that a ghost would not come and find me that night. From all of the stories I had heard, from all of the lore that surrounded any sort of physical proof that paranormal activities existed, I fell into the fear that accompanied it all. In order to understand the true fear that I felt for the notion of paranormal beings when trying to sleep at night, I'd like to share just one example. I am certain that it is not one that is unique to me, for my fear was only the by-product of the fear that was present amongst every other person I knew that were my age as a general term at that time. We fear what we do not understand. By the sheer biological nature that a human exists in a live state, we are not meant to understand the concept of a ghost in a non-living state.

Separately to prove this, one might ultimately fear death because there is a certain lack of knowledge that accompanies its existence. And there always will be. Upon the arrival of one's death, most begin to imagine it as some experience that can be looked down upon, as though from the view of a bird's eye. Even the arts depict this scene as such. To say that Death is something that can be looked at from a real vantage point, as if the person experiencing it had somehow managed to allow their perception to switch from their eyes to another location, is of course, folly. When Death rolls around, the person experiencing it does so from their own body. It is not something that one can describe, for it is something that one does not venture back from. It is final, and largely, I'd like to believe that this is the main reasoning why it is the thing that is feared the most commonly by the entire human race. It is interesting to think that it is something so unknown and so feared, and yet, something that everyone shall experience.

The example I'd like to present to describe my fear of ghosts when I was a child, is something that can be somewhat related to the fear of death, for there had been many a night that passed struggling to breath fresh air underneath the covers in my bed. I am surprised that in my attempts to evade any unwanted visitors, no harm came to me. It is quite possible that I myself should have died most nights in trying to sleep. For some reason, I cannot explain, I had always believed that the chances of a ghost visiting in the evening would be brought down to almost nothing if as many body parts as possible were covered by the sheets. If it was not visible to any passerby, then it would not be visible to any ghosts. Carrying this idea further, it was the utmost importance that the ears were covered, for if my ears were covered, no one would be able to whisper into them. One of my biggest fears centered largely on just this. I feared that one night, I would be lying in my bed trying to sleep and someone would whisper in my ear. A ghost would whisper into my ear.

In the present day, I recall this notion of fear with much amusement. A part of me wished largely still, that it was possible for me to feel the way I used to about ghosts. To fear something that I did not know beyond reason. The ghosts that haunted me now were far too real. They festered in the darkest and deepest parts of my soul like the plague, slowly eating away, slowly rotting every essence of life that I had ever thought pleasurable.

Most nights I find much difficulty in sleeping. Not due to the fear of a supernatural being that may or may not visit me, but from the ones that are always constantly there. Constantly in my mind, constantly telling me, whispering about every single detail of my life, every regret in full detail running over and over again. It was only by this that I understood what it truly meant to be afraid of ghosts. I wished in all honestly, that someone would have informed me that the ghosts I would have ended up fearing were the ones that I created all on my own. The ones that didn't exist, yet were are all too real. The ones that follow me around wherever my sombre body may lurk, the ones that sit with me at the dinner table, the ones that fuel my actions, and the ones that will ultimately, plunge me into a maddening darkness.

They follow me around, these whispers. They tell me discouraging things, always ensuring that I feel exhausted by the end of the day, absolutely tired to be in my own skin. They lurk in the darkest of shadows, and always succeed at dragging my weak mind with them. I hate these ghosts, these whispers of my past lives. Telling me constantly what I have done wrong, constantly making me wonder about what might have been had I done something differently, or said something different. It makes me sick, it keeps me from living my life the way that I'd like too, it keeps me from believing that I have any sort of tangible future, and most importantly, I believe largely that they are somewhat to blame for my inability to have been presented as a fellow vision of perfection to Vergil, as he did to me. For if they had never existed, they would never have influenced any sort of aspect in my life, and I might have more easily acted myself and the way I wanted to around him. Without considering every outcome, and its side effects, my life could have been so different. It could have been so much better, if I hadn't listened to these whispers, if I simply followed my heart. Vergil remains still as the freshest of the ghosts. I cannot shake him from my mind, even now, with the passing of time, as I want to.

To think about him is slowly and surely causing my mental ailments to transpire as physical pain and sickness. He haunts me. He is constantly in my mind, constantly in my thoughts, constantly a part of my life. I have only come to realize this in his absence. It was something I noticed when we had still been acquaintances, and only in his parting that my suspicions have been confirmed. To feel as though a part of yourself is gone is the most terrible feeling to have. In our parting it seems that I have experienced a level of sadness that I personally, had not known was possible for a human to experience. Of course these feelings have only been accentuated in my mind and it's morphing of him. So much time has passed since I last laid eyes on him, and yet, there has not been a day that has passed where I have not fallen asleep thinking about him. He has my thoughts; he is the ghost that whispers into my ear every night.

It humours me to think that even so, I am not afraid. If my only remembrance of him is to be in the past, then surely my mind would have let him go by now. No, I believe that there has to be something more to the entire situation. No one haunted me the way that he does. He has festered into the most personal parts of my brain. I know now what this meant. It meant that there was something more to this story, to the feelings that he made me feel. There was just simply something more. There had to be, for it made only logical sense for there to have been. For it to have been only small chapter in my life was a fact that I could not come to validate for it was not one that made sense. He was meant to be this ghost. He was meant to be the one that haunted me. Fate foretold this long ago.

Everything about the whole situation seemed to have unfolded too perfectly for it to have been otherwise. I believed what I believed and every night only further confirmed my feelings. It was in the darkest of the hours, in the calmest of the night that he would come and find me. Often I asked myself to what purpose, and I understood only that it was in love. The love that I had for this man was one that haunted me because I loved him more than myself.

I have begun at least for now, with the hopes of distracting my mind from him, to search for some sort of tangible supernatural being in my midst. If I could just be able to provide an example of an instance where a tangible ghost had contacted me, I feel as though my focus might be given the opportunity to shift away from him. I did not enjoy feeling as though my entire self had no control over anything, but that was exactly how he made me feel. At least a real ghost might have only controlled the level of fear that I experienced. He controlled my life, my existence. Everything I did, every minute I spent at work, every minute I spent lying awake at night, every item of clothing I bought, and every word that I chose to speak, he controlled. I knew this meant something, and I hoped that one day, I might be able to figure out what it was.

Speaking about the whole concept of ghosts, I believe it to be one of great ambiguity. A ghost really, in the end, is entirely a concept that is what you make of it. I know of people who choose not to take part in believing any type of supernatural being exists, and for whatever reason, have successfully gone their entire lives in believing this. I however, am not one of those people, and it seems, that even from the very beginning, there was something in my mind that has kept me from believing that it was not possible for ghosts, of whatever sort, to exist. Sometimes, I'd like to believe that all of my beliefs on the subject end with Vergil, for it makes sense to me that he was the answer to why I had been so afraid all along. If it was to end with him, then the ending I suppose, would ultimately be just that, an ending to all of my fear, to everything that I had ever feared. I would not feel as I do about him if I had not these previously established fears, and I might never have come to any conclusion about whether or not he had something to do with the reason for my existence.

Tears

Currently, there is only one wish that I had as a child that came true as an adult which I regret. I have heard the phrase "be careful what you wish for" many times before, but never had I actually thought that a day would come where I would have any sentiments of regret towards a wish I had as a child. Strangely enough, somewhere between all of the confusion of growing up, I wished for something that I never actually thought would come true to begin with. Now that it has, I feel both happy and sad. It is a strange feeling to regret something, especially something as silly as having the ability to cry on demand.

Growing up, I saw many different and astonishing actors and other people of fame that had the ability to cry on demand. I was simply taken aback by the whole idea. At first, I believed that these people were simply sad, which was also the explanation as to why they had been crying. Sadly enough, I know the exact opposite to be true now. As I can imagine, the people that I saw, the people that I wished to grow up and act just like, all had training to do so. I have had no such training, yet I have now my wish.

Within my intentions, I am not one to cry frequently. If I am sad, or am experiencing an uncontainable amount of pain, most of the time I will not cry. That is just the way that I am, since I see no reasoning that might have influenced this aspect of my life. Even as a child, my mother told me the story of how she pierced my ears when I was a baby and was astonished that I did not cry, I simply looked at her. I might have been expressing the pain I was experiencing through my stare, but I cannot conclude this validly, for it was is not a story that I have told, but rather one that was told to me. Even so, the fact remained that I did not cry all that much growing up, not like others that I knew.

Now, as the recipe goes, I need only to think of you Vergil, to think of the time that passed knowing you, and how it only exists now only as a memory. I try to understand that no matter how much the world changes and no matter how much I change, or even how much you do, forever the time and memories I've labelled as having occurred when I knew you are all ones that will never change. They will stay the same, and if time allows such actions, fester into the smallest crevices of my soul. Truthfully, as soon as a think of you, all your magnificence, your emptiness, and your uncertainty, there is something inside me that jumps. More times than not, I am plunged into this immeasurable sadness without even submitting my will to it. This whole thing, this whole small and significant fragment of my life has now been figured out. I can say without any falter now that I truly did love you Vergil.

If order means anything in the world, I have come to understand it as ironically as it might have ever hoped to have been presented to any living person. In reality, I wished to have the ability to cry before I met you, and in having met you I now have developed such an ability, of course only at the cost of my soul forever being lost without you in this life. On a linear scale, I understand such an order to be something that I never had the hopes of controlling to begin with. I had wanted something before I met Vergil, and now the wish that I had prior to the unravelling of these events has come true.

Sometimes, I like to pander to my own mind and claim that since I had wanted something before I met him, and by the end of it all I had achieved it, then surely if I had never wished such a thing in the first place, our love might have concluded differently than it did. I search often of reasons to blame on this misfortune; I try to find any sort of explanation, and consolation to help me sleep at night and function during the day. Some days it is easier to do than others. Most days I simply sit and stare at things as I have noted before, purely going over it all again and again in my mind. Thinking and laughing in madness at the thought that in the end my wish had come true and that of course it was Vergil that had allowed it to do so. So surreal, so unnerving. It is in the end, what it is. I may not have the ability to change things now, for I have only the ability to cry at the thought of living the rest of my life without ever seeing him, without ever hearing the sound of his voice, without ever touching his skin, without ever embracing his welcoming sent, and lastly, without ever tasting him again.

Afterword

I believe, even though I am still considered to be in my years of youth, that I have already committed the one mistake that will come to define me as a human being for the rest of my life. Such a revolutionary moment might definitely be taken seriously when the affected area in question is that of the soul. Simply from knowing that it is a commodity of value that can be bartered to the Devil, or even obtained by him through a considerably more socially acceptable method, I might come to the conclusion that it is something of value. Something of value. What an interesting concept. Let us investigate it a bit more thoroughly. What might something that is universally considered of value be to the average individual? Certainly, the soul is the most universally applicable concept I can think of. I would say in general, when paired with the sheer human natural instinct of self-preservation, the presence of a soul might simply be the reasoning for this.

In complete honesty it has now, with the elapsing of time, become difficult for me to express the words and message I have been trying to convey. I have not considered the implications of trying to understand what is possibly fuelling me to write this. I sit here writing and thinking in large majority exactly how upset it makes me every time I understand exactly how vital it is for me to complete this. I feel almost forced, inclined to do so. I was not given a choice, and it is this sheer lack of choice that my conscious self is upset with. It is the knowledge that I truly deep down do not feel as though I have really had any sort of say in the execution of this task. I feel simply that I was predetermined, predestined to do it and I have only the option of wondering why. I don't enjoy the fact that I was not really given a choice in the matter, because I would not be doing this if I it was solely up to me. However, now that I have come to terms with the fact that it must be done, I want to finish it now more than ever. For every day that passes, another day fills it place with an atmosphere even more sombre and unforgiving than the last. Awoken days are instantly filled with sadness and the inability to come to terms with the fact that my life must be lived without having a chance to explain it all to you Vergil. Even though I have come to terms with the impact that I was unable to establish myself as an importance within your existence, I still wondered about, and hoped internally, that it would be different.

This has made more sense to me than anything I have ever consciously known before. As a child I bore witness to countless stories of unconditional love, about princesses finding their princes, about the ability for true love to conquer anything. It does not seem absurd to me to expand on the notion of it being possible for true love to recollect ones soul from the Devil after he, by whatever means, had acquired it. If one loses his soul to the Devil through choosing to take his own life, is it possible to break such a contract with true love? I can only hope so.

For being an individual whom knows not tangibly what love even is, I find it very difficult to fight for something that I have never known. I know only the jump through my blood that my heart makes every time I think about Vergil losing his soul to the Devil wrongly. To say wrongly, I simply mean in unknowing ignorance. For I believe that throughout the development of its lives, a soul might validly come to the conclusion that making the trade of their soul to the Devil in exchange for some other sought after commodity might be worth it. I see how a naïve, maybe even relatively new soul, could do this. However, I do believe also that in this one moment of weakness it is not simply acceptable for the Devil to so carelessly agree to this deal without considering the other soul that goes with the soul being lost. I understand that this is simply the kind of business that he chooses to do, not only because he has the power to do so, but also because simply, it is a business that will always have quite a large customer margin. When you have the monopoly on such activities and you're the best person for the job, it really only seems logical for such a business to be yours.

It is not in the loosing of one's soul that has made be upset. It is the sheer fact that I believe his soul should never even have been given the option of getting lost. It always had a home, it existed within my soul, and I am now at a loss. The fact that he lost it based on a simple technicality is one that I cannot overlook. That seems like a might grey zone to me. For even on a business level, a product cannot be sold if the commodity in question has already been sold. Something cannot be sold twice. Therefore, when speaking about the commodity being a soul, I'd like to think equally that this cannot be an exchange if its validity can questioned so easily.

Completion and Contemplation

I must admit something about myself. It is a fact that I have known for a while and it is a bit scary to write down in fact. I have never really completed anything in my life. I have never really followed through on anything or said that I have gotten to the last of something. I have so many lipsticks that are half used; I've never even come to finished one. I don't know why. It's a kind of weird thing that I do and have done, without even realizing that it is actually only me that does this.

Honestly I cannot conclusively say that if I had managed to succeed in finishing this, which in all its actuality is perfect, I would say that largely, that I could attribute all this to you perhaps. I mean again, perhaps it is largely more a reflection of the author than of the person in which the author has written about, but can we surely be certain? I think not, based on the fact that the completion of this book from beginning to end would mean that it would never have existed if I had not met you and to me that must mean something or at least it would seem to be as having been significant to this whole affair in the first place. I guess that since such a conclusion is concrete now, this is exactly what it was meant to be.

In conclusion I have only this to say Vergil. So much time has passed and yet a day does not go by where I can say that I have not thought about you, about where you might be in your life, and about how happy you may be. I still have not come to know the exact reason why I have been so inclined to writing this story of love, but I guess you could say that I owe it to the girl that existed once, who believed that you were absolutely the best thing ever to have existed on this planet. I owe this to the girl who, no matter how many times you knocked down, believed only that you were destined for greatness. It upsets me to understand that this girl existed once upon a time, and nothing more. Currently, I am reminded only of the fact that despite my best attempts, I was never what you wanted. I was never good enough in the time that we knew each other.

If it means anything to you, know this. I worry constantly about you, and think constantly about you. I have heard others speak of your affect, saying that you have since my knowing you, come to live as a changed man. Of course, I take their word on these accusations for I have not seen you since I realized I was in love with you. I believe that one day you might feel differently, you might be a happy man. It makes my insides curdle to think that such a moment might come to you in the arms of another. I know no one could ever be able to have the same impact on me as you had. As I understand it, I wish for this story in its entirety to serve only one purpose, and that is as one of hope. Never was there a true moment that passed in my mind where I believed you to have been a lost soul for eternity. I believe Vergil that you once did have a soul and that perhaps if time has allowed it to be so, you shall have it returned to you soon.

I walked up the stairs and thought to myself, if I had anything I had this. This would be the only thing I could ever say that I completed. Perhaps it will be the start of great things to come, which could be possible, but I think more likely that the by-product here will be the short lived life of a girl who was simply not meant to exist within this lifetime; who has in some way, validly come to the conclusion that she might fare better taking her chances in another life.

That now, the task that I was meant to complete in my life had come to pass already. The God or Gods or whomever one might attribute life to, gave me the opportunity to exist within the confines of a body with the end goal of getting my dear soul mate his half back so we would both be able to move onto the next stage of our existences, and already it is clear as day to me that I have failed in completing such a task. I wish only now to spend every waking breath of my ill lived life in pursuing the man who remains without a soul, as cold as the body that functions under such circumstances. I had not, in all honesty, realized all the implications that would have been involved in this second chance of circumstance. I thought it might have been possible; to love one enough to the point where they might come to realize that a life of happiness was conceivable even if in they did not have their soul.

We both live without one another, and such a fact couldn't possibly fill my soul with anymore grief. It is not the grief that I cannot be with him; it is the grief that I believed I actually had a chance to mean something more in his life than all the other people of his past, present, and future. Now I remain here, living a life of solitude, hoping still with all my heart that if I work hard enough, if I put enough of my life into it, our paths might cross once more under different, more ideal, circumstances.

Before I met you, I never truly believed that it was possible for me to feel as though I had anything that I could tangibly say was mine from start to finish. And although, I have not the ability to conclude such a thing about you my love, I can say such things validly about the love presented within these pages. You exist within these pages forever as the one that belongs to me. Largely, I understand the story as the by-product of my mind, but simply because such a fact is so, it does not mean that it is not real. I completed something entirely for you Vergil, and I am not afraid in the least to say so. The defining moment of my life had finally come. I have accomplished something in my life; the only thing I can say I have ever completed from start to finish. It seems that the answer of what to do after its completion did not surface to my brain. Lastly, I did not get sad that such an opportunity was over, but I was glad that it had happened. A life well lived is a life that was not wasted, and I can say that I have lived well.

Did I honestly believe in my heart of hearts that it was possible for me to complete this? Yes I did. In fact, I saw it as clear as day. I believed that you made it possible for me to have this tangible piece of work. Honestly, if I may thank you for anything, it is for making it possible for you to always have been the one that made it possible. Had our souls had been intertwined from the start? Well, I think about the situation as I will always. That I will forever be in your gratitude for allowing me to exist as the creator of this affair. I am flattered. I wanted to have the possibility of being a significant part in history and I do not know anyone who, in their right, or even left mind, would be able to refuse an offer as delectable as being able to exist as a human and also an extension of time, in history. Another point seems to be proven. I shall go down in time as that, and you as this and it will forever be known as such. It has taken a lot for me to finish this, and it should be known exactly just how much the completion of this book means to me. It is significant and your are significant because I wished for you to be significant. You mattered to me and I'd like for it this to let it be recognizable that I did it; I have something to call my own. Thank you for making this possible, you will always have my heart.

My mind has come to find much difficulty in deciding what the next step to take in my life should be. I want nothing more than to be with you, to get not only your soul back for you from the Devil, but to open the option of moving onto the next part of life for my soul, is one that is also apparent. It seems that I am stuck between no more than these two decisions. The first, being of course, more grim and final than the other.

Even if I am successful in all of this; if I succeed in getting Vergil his soul back, I am certain that I will still not be able to be with him in this life. To return ones soul when half of the current life has already come to pass without it would certainly be more detrimental than having the soul taken away in the first place. How would one even know how to live in such a state? The returning of his soul seemed also to be a sort of action that would be performed only in the intermittent stages between lives. Therefore, no matter what level of success I have in getting his soul back, The option for us to be together would only ever surface in the next life.

It is in this fact that I have now come to question my own life, and whether or not it is worth living beyond this point. I have the option of living the rest of my life out, constantly in the wake of regret and sorrow, working only on things that might get my love's soul back, or I can marvel at the work that I have completed here for him already in trying to get his soul returned. Do I want to choose to live in illness and without even the option of loving my soul mate for the rest of my life? I find this to be a fate worth considering as being even worse than living a life without one's soul. For, if one is living without a soul, then surely they haven't the knowledge of what they are missing out on because it was something they never had to begin with. Just as I may never know what it would be like to live a life where I actually succeeded in being able to be with the other half of my soul and with you Vergil, my love.

The first option remains as choosing to take my own life. It is not the option that I find most preferable, for it involves my soul remaining in Hell for the rest of eternity, but it is the option that would allow our souls to be reunited once more, even if it meant that the Devil would have his way in the end. I have never been one for patience and the sheer fact that I would have to live out the rest of my life, then wait until the circumstances to be with Vergil to arise in the future is the option that I find much harder to choose. I want to be with him, I want to have the option of saying that I successfully completed my soul, that beyond all doubts and obstacles, I did it. To wait until the next life might the hardest thing that I have ever been faced with doing. I do not want to wait. Even if this is all real, even if it isn't just a series of circumstances that have festered in my mind to the point of belief, there is no sure guarantee that in the next life I would succeed in assuring the return of his soul.

Killing myself then, seems to be the most suitable option. It makes sense in my logical mind to do so. I would not have to live without my love or within the shameful body that I have been given. I would get to exist in the state of perfection that I have come to know as my soul and would be able to spend it with you. Two things of perfection that come only at the price of spending it as such for the rest of eternity, in a flaming inferno. The cost it seems, is outnumbered by the benefits I might receive from buying such an action. I can live out the rest of my life without Vergil and try to move on, try to live on as he did without me in the past, or I can take the same route he did, fermenting only the facts of just how certain I am that it was the same soul we originated from.

The story that I have told here is one that I hope is strong enough to hold up to the test of time. Time has taken away many a thing from me, and tarnished many a life's opportunity. I do not want to give up on the one thing that I have ever come to believe as worth doing. Time has not been kind to me. I do not believe that it ever was however, and so its gestures come as no surprise to be. I am committed to the ending that I know shall come to my soul one day. Even if it is not in this life, I know it shall come to me one day and that I shall have another chance at happiness. I wish nothing but the best for Vergil, and I have nothing but love and the rest of my soul for him. I never believed for a moment that I had the chance of fulfilling my soul's goal in this life, but I do believe that I have been given the ability to try my absolute best. If this life should come only as a failure, an intermittent period of sorrow, then let it be known as such.

Within the confinements of this life, or this contract, I did not come to realize, I think, the full extent of just how difficult and filled with emotions this life would be. I have come to understand that in living this life without his soul, Vergil has suffered severe changes in his disposition towards life in general. I did not realize just how cold and lacking of emotions he was to be in this life when I agreed to its conditions. I accepted these terms and condition, knowing that I had the opportunity to get him back, to get his soul back, but just as he lives without his soul now, I live without him.

It has been in the past now for a while, and still not a single moment goes by where it does not pain me to think about how we will never be together. I understand the circumstances around the fact's explanation, but I guess I just choose ultimately to believe that it didn't really matter what reality told me, I knew what I felt. And that was enough for me. I wanted this to go down as the first thing that I have ever completed, and that it was completed only because I had met you. That is one Hell of a conclusion to make, but now that we have reached the end, I find it the only valid one that can be so.

I am proudest in this moment. I have completed something of tangible significance. Yes, it feels great to be done this, these moments. It is only in completion that I realized what finishing this actually meant. I had no other option. It was the thing that I was meant to do; the thing that had to be done. Literally, I needed for this to have been the significant thing in my life. It would have been and for eternities will continue to be the thing that I couldn't have bared continued doing. Simply knowing you caused me physical, mental, and soulful pain. I couldn't have you, and that does make sense to me now. I was never meant to have you. Ah, simply because that's just how it was written in time.

Perhaps it would not be too silly of a notion to suppose that I have succeeded in completing something because I knew you. Your existence in my life was one that was destined to finish. I felt only pain in knowing that I would only ever be a small insignificant fraction of your life, and you be such a large and significant part of mine. I find a small amount of humour in it however, because isn't that just exactly the way it is for most type of things? There are always two different realties. There's the one where you are the one writes the story about another, and the one where you are the story's main subject. I guess I never really thought I would be the one that ended up with the initial of the two.

At times, I have smiled with a smirk on my face, laughing also to myself because I know that I am still quite young and I'd like to think of myself how one usually thinks of good wine. I was only to get better with age; at least for now. If you take little steps each day, no matter how big a step, it is still one in the right direction. I felt great taking this step, saying that this part of my life that existed and centered around knowing you is over. I realize now just how much I was truly enthralled by you. I wish it could have lasted; or rather you would have given me a shot. And as much as I would like to close with a sentence that would prove that you never meant anything to me, such a sentence is not one, which by the sheer existence of this book, that I believe anyone can make.

The feelings of euphoria and perfection that I feel in this moment are absolutely and utterly fantastic. What a relief it is to finally say that I am done feeling so tender and impoverished all the time, feeling upset that I could never finish anything or call myself something of significance. But alas, here it is, staring back at me, I am significant. You are significant. We exist as remaining significant together and forever. But it is just something that shall exist in time, and not in my life. I shall continue to live this life and go on to either make it absolutely meaningless, or very meaningful. I guess in having known you, the latter has now become an option that was not known before. I smile.

In this moment of solace, I feel that I shall never cry another tear for you. It is somewhat comforting to know that I can say that I am finished with this. I have finished this. I am done with thinking about these feelings, of believing in something other than that believing in anything was absolutely stupid and pointless. It is stupid that I believed in you because you have let me down more than I can describe. I thought for sure this was going to be the life that I would have been able to call you, even if only for a short period of life, my own. It is not all terrible to be somewhat generally unhealthy. I like to think of it as a blessing in disguise because it makes me want to live my life a little bit more than to the fullest, to be the best that I can be. To only get better as time goes on, because it will go on for me in much less a time than it will for anyone else. Now that I can say my life is not all that terrible, I feel a small amount of relief. The story is over and I shall no longer cry about this.

I get to move on to the next part of my life, to make it worth as much as possible. And you are forever fragmented in time as a magnificent being; no longer shall you not be feel able to accept the temptations in life that led to shape the way our minds work, you are perfect, and I'd like for it be known as such. You do not ever need to feel like you are not a good person, or that you do not deserve the love of others. No one deserves that. I see your perfection as concretely as the world could have described it. Oh well, I do believe concretely now also, that there is more than likely a chance that I might have the prospect to be with you in another lifetime.

Sometimes things are just as they are meant to me, and that is simply life. But I would have been damned in this one to an eternity of regret if I didn't complete this. Not knowing whether or not I really did give it my best shot is something that I cannot afford in this lifetime. You are connected to my soul and to not be able to have you is absolutely a break in the line of my soul and my life, but like I have said, it is not one that has ever surprised me. When the mind, body, and soul all experience distress at the same time, they all suffer. I really do believe that if I would have continued to have known you, it would surely have killed me; slowly, bitterly, and painfully.

Of course, I look forward to meeting you again, in the next life in which the contract allows us to meet. Perhaps I will have learned to wait, where regret, or lack of it, would be the only two outcomes that weigh any amount of significance to me. Until the next life, my love.